Betrayer

Scourge of Trabonus

Beware who comes knocking.
On planet Tora, murder has a silent partner.

Novella 2

Yuan Jur

Cover art : Ralph Manis/Infinitee Designs

Australia

Betrayer by Yuan Jur

ISBN-13: 978-0-9942153-1-4 (Paperback)
ISBN-13: 978-0-6481977-9-9 (E-Book Epub)
ISBN-13: 978-0-9942153-5-2 (E-Book MOBI)

Cover and art design by Ralph Hawke Manis of Infinitee Designs 2017
www.infinitee-designs.com
Book design and production by WaaDoom in association with
Thebookpatch.com
Editing and structure by Charles Wannop and De Chao Peterson

Dedication

Many thanks to the Citadel 7 series Crew.

Editors John David Kudrick & Mary Rosenblum, Charles Wannop, the many proof readers and the beta test group who help the Citadel 7 series reach for the high bar.

Orders

"Welcome Agent. This mission propels us along the Superverse continuum through the endless oceans of Dark Matter. We will emerge in a timeline where some things will seem familiar, others quite strange. The voice of *Central* will now take you through our brief. See you on the ground. Mission success to us all!"

C-DATE: CLASSIFIED.
UNFOLDING TIMELINE: ACTIVE.
REGION OF CONTACT: CELESTIAL ENDLESS ZONE.
ERA: POST SECOND CITADEL WAR.
CLASSIFIED PLANET SECURITY LEVEL: 10.
IDENTIFICATION: T . . . T . . . TORA.
ERROR!
SYSTEM HIJACKED!
REROUTING—STAND BY.

"Human Agent, are you there? Naught's beard! This better work. Gods damn this Jenaoin technology. Ehhh . . . What does this one do? Where is a competent servant when you need one? Ah, this should do it.

"Agent, my name is Evercycle Three. My designation is 'Lord of Chaos.' I don't have much time before Central identifies my signal and severs this hijack. Yes yes, I know it *looks* like a page in a book to you, but it's much more. Just shut up and read. What I'm about to tell you will keep you safe—will give you *and* freedom a chance. A great miscarriage of justice has occurred. My son, Herrex, Lord of Balance, has been wrongly imprisoned on the world of Tora.

***

"They are sending you to Tora now to make certain you are misled. It is part of a greater plan for dominating existence. Herrex is blamed for a great many things. Not all are his doing. It was a misdemeanor or two . . . nothing more than some insignificant worlds repurposed, I assure you. Yes, he is impetuous at times and difficult to reason with. But the true deceiver—and a great danger to us all—is working behind the scenes. So my son is angry, Agent, and looking for escape. He feels betrayed by everyone and intends revenge.

"A huge cover-up is underway. Those who wear the halo of good are not all they seem. The existence of many is at stake. Even though you are not aligned to my house, I beg you to be just in your verdict. What you decide may carry the day. Not unlike your Earth, Tora has great landmasses and diverse races . . . even technology, of a kind. Its planetary mass was created at the same time as your world, only in another dimension. Both worlds, though, were brought into being for the same cursed reason. Did they explain any of this to you?

"Anyway, just don't believe what you hear of my Herrex from your, uh . . . allies. It's all lies. See for yourself, and I'll let you decide. Change had to come to put things right; that's all Herrex was trying to do. A few thousand worlds were lost, but that was unavoidable. He didn't mean it. His actions were just . . . misunderstood. Your race has more in common with my Herrex than you know, Agent. One way or another, we are now all integral to this one vast multiverse.

"Your transition to Tora is at hand. Be careful when your feet touch ground. Tora is a level-ten security world—a place where none get in or out without approval scans and special permission. Only those wardens of the House of Zero are exempt. They may come to check on Herrex as they need, but no one else. Well . . . there is one other possible exception, and his sympathies lie with me. Otherwise Tora is off the grid from the discoverable time-space Continuum for now. Herrex may have been excessive in some of his actions, but he didn't deserve this.

"The balance of power in Superverse evolution has to change. I have plans in place to see that this occurs, and soon. As you descend, look directly below and you will see there breathes the Flaxon city of Weirawind. Amidst its soft, flickering lamp lights and burning street braziers, buildings huddle together like tidy, fortified mounds of brick and wood. The citizens living along its stone-paved streets aspire to many things, as simple mortals go. They are steered by a blind church belief in only one god, and governed by a dynasty of ruthless despots looking for the next best power play. You need to know that they are militant toward any race not under their thumb. Your Earth history has had its share of despots too, hasn't it? Earth's Napoleonic period would compare well to the culture and ruling class of Flaxor, only their leader is one Regent Trabonus. They have a cunning written and spoken language. They also have a disciplined military on foot and horseback.

"I urge you to start your journey by observing the actions of the Flaxon ruler. Trust no one, Agent. Nothing is as it seems."

CHAPTER

1

Schemes Aplenty

Regent Trabonus looked out on Weirawind City's southern aspect from his recently refurbished War Room. In deep thought the lord and master of Flaxor stared at the storming night skies through open shutters from the third story. Slanting sheets of rain still pelted down from the day before, chilled by the eastbound winds of leaf-fall. Slate-gray clouds bristled with an electric light show from within, echoing the present situation needling the regent's mind.

Holding the broad lapels of his favorite black gambeson, Trabonus watched a flash of lightning strike the ground in the forest far to the south. The dull glow of the subsequent fire died quickly in the persistent downpour. Trabonus contemplated the recent strife between his brother, Magistrate Waldon the Elder, and himself, even as servants milled about behind him in silence. The regent scratched the stubble of his ongoing but futile attempt to grow a beard, and then he sighed.

So there is little choice in the matter. How will I handle this?

To his left, at the servery on the far side of the war table, his butler set down a tray. On it was hot char, a carafe of wine, and some light supper for those soon to arrive.

The pleasant peppery smell of burning needle bush and stendle wood stimulated Trabonus's rather bulbous, hairy nose. He flared his nostrils, considering with some annoyance the tiny flaws in the new textiles and floor coverings recently installed in the refurbishment.

Perhaps an afternoon of energetic flogging would help me think clearer. There must be more transgressors the jailer could round up.

His focus returned to his new surroundings. The rug makers had delivered the new wall hangings and patterned floor coverings only that afternoon. The new stitch work on the tapestries from the master weaver looked tolerable this time, Trabonus had told them on inspection.

I think I'll order an extra barrel of mead for the master weaver. And perhaps order that the rug makers are given leisure for half a day this moon too. My benevolence knows no bounds. Hmm . . . definitely warmer in here now since I had the flue remade.

"You there," Trabonus called to a passing servant. "See another solid piece goes on the fire before we begin."

"As you wish, my lord."

The subject matter—and resulting mood—will bring a chill of its own, I've no doubt.

Now seeing his thirty-eighth season of leaf-fall, Trabonus mused that much had transpired since his father's untimely passing and his own succession to the regency. It was something that had taken the military junta by surprise, since Trabonus's older brother, Waldon, had been next in line. Yet it had been Waldon himself who made the announcement, though many who knew him well saw and heard the indignation in his delivery. It had also been common knowledge that Waldon was the favorite of their father, Straxus II. Trabonus had arrived into the world almost killing his mother at birth. Lady Morgania nonetheless declared him the miracle Flaxor was destined to have. As a child and teenager, the young Trabonus quickly earned the whispered name of "Little Mr. Never Wrong" amongst castle staff. "No" was the most uncommon word that Trabonus heard whilst his father was out of eye and ear shot. His mother forgave his every transgression, of which there were a multitude, and punished severely any who would bar his way. Morgania's flagrant disregard for her husband's directive—to discipline their younger son in his absence—was always met with forceful consequences upon his return. Thus Trabonus hated his father, and at the banquet of his Coming of Age—in a supposed drunken stupor—he openly vowed to return the favor.

Some moons later, while Trabonus was away being educated in trade and commerce, his father, mother, and brother went on a private hunt. Castle staff later heard from one of the hunting party's chasers that Lady Morgania's mount missed a jump and threw her violently to ground. "The accident saw her neck broken on the spot," the chaser said.

On Trabonus's return the news propelled him into a rage—and a witch hunt to have blame attributed. Soon enough Trabonus found a note from his mother addressed to him, saying she feared for her life. It suggested foul intentions on the part of his father and brother. While no clear proof could be established, after reading the note Trabonus began hating his father and brother equally.

Standing there now in his War Room, Trabonus's gut tightened while thinking on the subject as if it had happened only yesterday.

Father has paid . . . and Waldon, dear brother, you shall see a similar fate. Trabonus clenched his jaw. *Mother will not go unavenged. The moment I find that which you hold over me, my action will be swift.*

A servant padded up respectfully and offered a refreshment on a silver tray. Trabonus paid it momentary consideration and then, with a short shake of his head, dismissed the offering.

"The hearth and refreshment are ready for your guests, my lord," the servant said before bowing his head and retreating.

Trabonus had always been much stronger in parlor games and intrigue than battlefield prowess. That was Waldon's strength. The last significant coup Trabonus orchestrated saw him bypass his older brother and ascend to the regency. However, that didn't occur without being stalemated by Waldon. His brother had secured his own safety back then by implementing some devious blackmail. With that, Waldon demanded to be assigned the lesser, but not insignificant, power position of chief magistrate of Flaxor. This gave him theoretical control of the military. That position also by default handed him jurisdiction over the inner-city police force and, in principle, the Royal House Security. The RHS always operated as a sinister cluster of shadowy figures whose loyalty traditionally lay with the regent. Trabonus knew his brother valued control of the RHS most of all. However, the head of RHS operations —Terrance Blackly—ensured that a continued flow of reliable intelligence made its way to Trabonus, which Waldon knew about but could do nothing to stop.

Whispers in the Weirawind court spoke of Trabonus as a good catch in lands and titles, as long as a woman wore a blindfold and was happy to say "Yes" to his every utterance. She had to be indifferent to his daily foul, sour alcohol breath. She also had to accept that his idea of affection amounted to a one-sided liaison, usually as he fell on top of her, drunk. Finally she had to accept that he only felt compelled to bathe once every four passing seasons, whether he needed it or not. In exchange for accepting these minor individual quirks, Trabonus offered riches as positively the wealthiest Flaxon in Ludd. He always lavished the object of his affection with all that wealth could buy, unless he needed it back. She also had her own company of soldiers to take her anywhere she need to go, unless he needed them back. One thing was sure: Trabonus was not a Flaxon to be crossed or underestimated. His memory was long, and retribution toward his enemies knew no bounds.

Trabonus turned his gaze downward upon his newly tailored War Room attire, giving a small smile of satisfaction. The ensemble came complete with a never-drawn ceremonial sword on his right hip. It was clipped to a broad gilded belt that held up his fluted pantaloons. Most of all Trabonus admired his knee-high brown ealk-skin boots, which he personally had a hand in designing. Whispers in the court said he had an odd foot fetish.

So many untapped skills, he thought, rubbing the toe of his left boot on the calf of his right. *They'll be the height of court fashion, no question. Is there nothing I cannot achieve?*

He imagined some whimsical grand portrait of himself, wearing these very same boots at battle's end while astride a white thoroughbred.

Head held high, I think. Triumphant amidst the ruins of a Scarzen bunker.

A flash of lightning and two more cracks of thunder broke his musings and drew his view south.

"With any luck more Scarzen will be dead over there tonight," he whispered to himself.

Then, for a moment, he thought he heard the faintest sinister chuckle in the far distance.

"Hmph," he muttered. "Sometimes the clouds behave as if they have a will of their own, I'm sure of it."

"Everything alright, my lord?" asked a servant standing close by.

Trabonus turned to look at the middle-aged servant. "What? Oh . . . no, I'm fine. See to your duties."

Then Trabonus looked back to the storm. *Would that I had such power, Ludd would be ruled as it should be, as the Maker intended—with me guiding its course.*

Behind him servants opened the tall carved timber doors to the War Room. Trabonus turned to see who had arrived. Several representatives of Weirawind City's most influential Flaxon hierarchy entered. Striding in, the silver-haired Magistrate Waldon led the procession. An aide followed on his heels, carrying a documents satchel.

Waldon removed his tricorn hat and clutched it under an arm, giving his brother a steely look while paying the minimal drop of his head in respect.

Not far behind Waldon the head of the Flaxon church, Archbishop Magnus Targus, filled the doorway. His long, gaunt face and stony expression gave little away, as always. Full-length crimson robes resembling just-hung tapestry left only the bishop's face and hands exposed. Magnus Targus bowed toward Trabonus politely, tall hat still on his head, and then he moved off to his usual seat.

Next, bringing some dignity to the room, came Colonel Ferdinand Hitex, commander of Flaxor's military. A striking figure of a senior Flaxon officer, Colonel Hitex wore grubby white riding trousers, a blue gambeson, and dirty black boots—testimony of him having just returned from a military exercise. Regardless of his journey, Hitex looked unruffled, as was his norm. Like Magistrate Waldon the silver-haired Hitex carried his tricorn hat under one arm.

Taking a couple of strides forward, Hitex stopped. He snapped his heels together with discipline and then presented a salute of his right fist across the heart, along with a shallow bow. Trabonus noticed the gold buttons of Hitex's blue gambeson glistened in the glow of the hearth firelight, then the regent acknowledged him with a slight nod. Hitex moved to the near end of the table and took his appointed seat assisted by a servant.

Finally, bringing a chill to the room of his own, Terrence Blackly entered. Clad in a standard RHS shin-length gray coat and trousers, he looked able to blend in with any shadow, despite being a heavy-set fellow. Holding his derby hat in hand, Blackly showed some stubble on an ordinarily shaven chin, suggesting he'd been traveling rough. After bowing to Trabonus, Blackly stood fast, waiting to be directed by his regent. Trabonus acknowledged him and waved Blackly on. He moved to his seat opposite Colonel Hitex.

Hitex slung Blackly a disapproving glance. "No time for ablutions, Blackly?"

Blackly took one look at Hitex and said, "I see you have had much the same chance, sir."

Interrupting their exchange, a servant approached each of the guests with refreshments.

Meanwhile Waldon directed his aide to place the satchel at his seat at the War Table. Waldon then moved off to the refreshments servery and poured himself a goblet of wine before approaching Trabonus.

"You wasted no time in summoning us after your last disappearing act," Waldon said, then took a sip of the honey-colored liquid. "I see your faithful hound Blackly has returned. Brought back some scraps for you to frustrate over, has he?"

Trabonus presented a steely glare and tightened jaw at Waldon.

"He won't find what you're seeking, you know," Waldon said. He shot a disdainful glance Blackly's way. "Poor fellow looks like he's been hiding under rocks and running from the Scarzen for his life again." Waldon smiled at his brother. "Aww, still can't find what is so elusive."

"Mind your tone, brother. Don't forget your rightful place."

Waldon patted the right side of his coat, which contained an inside pocket. "Oh, I haven't, little brother." Then Waldon noticed the others now paying attention to their whisperings whilst trying to feign disinterest.

"I'll see your head put to the block for your treachery," Trabonus said, slitting his eyes at his brother.

"You first," Waldon said with soft sarcasm. "Don't forget what will happen if I, my wife, or my children come to any grief. The proof—bearing your personal ring seal—I carry on my person at all times."

Trabonus reached out and grabbed Waldon's arm. Now Waldon knew he'd gotten to his brother.

"Unhand me," Waldon said, looking at the regent's hand on his arm.

Reluctant, Trabonus complied.

Waldon leaned in and whispered, "That poisonous little assassin may have gotten to Father, but he missed me. Now I have him in custody. He's safe, ready at a moment's notice to testify against you."

Trabonus unclipped his sword, clearly incensed. He held out the piece for a nearby servant to come collect.

"Put this in its place," Trabonus ordered. "And close all the shutters."

"Yes, my lord," replied the servant, taking the weapon and bowing.

Trabonus walked past his brother as if Waldon was never there and then headed for the table. After helping the regent into his seat, a servant placed a small silver bell on the table to his right. Trabonus looked at Blackly, who gave him an almost imperceptible nod. Then Trabonus drew a steady breath, hoping Blackly might have something to show for his absence this past moon.

"Servants may leave," Trabonus announced.

As the servants scurried off, the regent looked toward Waldon, who had moved to the fireplace. Staring into the flames, the magistrate seemed to be deliberately ignoring the others.

"Brother. Do come sit," Trabonus called. "You're brooding again. We've an expanding empire to run."

Waldon did as requested, though a cold reticence clearly accompanied him. Trabonus extracted an elegant flat silver tin from his vest pocket. From it he thumbed a pinch of snuff up his nose. A calamitous sneeze erupted from Trabonus into cupped hands. He took a used nose cloth from a trouser pocket and wiped his face, being sure to dig a finger well inside one hairy nostril to finish. While the bishop and Blackly redirected their point of view, Waldon and Colonel Hitex eyed the regent's common practice with contained umbrage.

Trabonus finished his disgusting habit, taking a moment to consider those at his table.

"Good sirs. Before we raise the question of further conquest across Ludd, let us press the trifles out of the way. How goes the ministration and expansion of trade for our fair Flaxor? Waldon, brother, why don't you begin."

Waldon took momentary pause to consider his next words. He pulled on the broad lapels of his silver-trimmed black vest. Then he took a parchment from the satchel in front of him and finally cleared his throat to speak.

"Taxes are steady, my lord. Coffers have ample sums to manage trade. But the regent's grain stocks are low. Additionally recent raids by the Scarzen on our domestic zukaa herds have cut our volume by 30 percent."

"Is that sustainable?" Bishop Targus asked.

"It is at present," Waldon replied. "But poaching of game in the regent's hunting grounds is a problem. The antler beast herds have become scarcer over the last ten moons. I recommend endorsing a need to cut back on the regular full-moon feasts if their numbers are to grow again."

"Nonsense," Trabonus said. "Our hardworking nobles need to let their hair down for looking after our revolting underclass. Send out patrols. Catch a poacher or two. Make a firm example of them in the main square, and offer reward to those with information leading to conviction. Don't actually pay the fools, of course."

Waldon sighed and moved on. "Poaching has caused some considerable losses. Stores will need to be well managed if we are to see the next leaf-fall and white-fall through. Next, crime is being managed within city walls to acceptable levels. The RHS report a Chou spy was apprehended and turned over to Mr. Blackly's cells for interrogation yesterday. I recommend we try to turn them first. If that fails, torture and information extraction—and a blind trade for the dead body—is acceptable . . . just as they have done to us in the past."

Fingers of one hand tapping the table, Trabonus looked at Blackly. "Will you be able to turn them, Blackly?"

"A Chou spy?" Blackly paused, then shrugged. "Difficult to say, my lord," he said in his husky tone. "They pride themselves in having the stamina to hold out against considerable persuasion. The last one wasn't forthcoming, apart from soiling himself before he was gutted on the dungeon block."

Blackly's tone sounded disappointed, thus drawing the colonel's gaze. So Blackly shot Hitex a glance. Seeing the colonel's obvious disdain for him, Blackly smartly ignored it, refocusing his view on Trabonus.

"Stubborn folk, those Chou," Trabonus said. "I'll be so pleased when their lands are in our hands and some civility seeded amongst their slant-eyed masses." He eyed his brother again. "Continue, Waldon."

"Only six hangings this moon, my lord," Waldon said. "From my observation public executions are losing their power. They just don't have the same shock value they did for your predecessor, my lord. Perhaps there might be more forward-thinking ways to keep the citizens in line."

Trabonus raised an eyebrow. "Like what? Giving the commoner an independent vote on who runs things? Really, next you'll be suggesting females should have equal say in court." His expression hardened. "They'll be pressed into submission or be left to fend for themselves in the land of the Scarzen demon."

"Rightly said, my lord," Blackly chimed in.

"Mark my words, gentlemen," Trabonus continued. "I'll not have the good name of Regent Straxus smeared in broad or close company while I lead this fair nation. Certainly not while investigations into his untimely death still proceed."

With those words Trabonus set his gaze on Waldon. The brothers locked stares for an uncomfortable short moment.

"All I'm saying," Waldon went on, "is we'll have to think of something else if we are going to keep their minds where we—uh . . . where *you'd* like them, my lord."

Soft and low in Trabonus's ear he heard the same voice he'd been hearing in his dreams of late: *"Give them bread and circuses while you play the real game."*

"Why not simply step up the pace on the games arena?" Trabonus asked. "Bring them sport and distraction. The suffering of beasts and enemies always helps lift their spirits. Away from that topic now. Tell me of the canal project. When shall I see my navy in harbor at Weirawind? And are the Celeron still barking over freshwater loss and taxes?"

Waldon nodded. "They are. They threaten embargo if we don't reconsider our terms. Their food trade supplements nearly 25 percent of the city's intake during the leaner moons. If you intend to ignore their request to at least parley, as you have done the past four seasons, I would expect retaliation. If I may remind you, we are fighting a war on three fronts outside our walls: one militarily and two politically. With last season's crop failures a consistent Celeron food supply is vital to the replenishment of our stores. We don't want to be fighting an internal rebellion with our citizens as well, not with that much in play."

"Let me guess, you have a suggestion to guard against such a rebellion?" Trabonus asked.

"I do, my lord. I thought we might cut back a little on the continuing oversupply of church silos. The priests have far more than their fair share."

"I agree," Colonel Hitex said. "Those stores could be put to far better use feeding the columns of my men in the field who patrol and protect our borders. My commanders have reported a decline in morale at being supplied only salted pork and boiled grain to fill our ranks' bellies. The overall health of your army is suffering, my lord. That directly affects the security of Flaxor."

Bishop Targus cleared his throat. "My lord, I must protest. The church's work takes considerable effort. My priests must have strength to exercise proper representation of the One *and* my lordship's interests across the land."

"You can't be serious," Hitex said. "You have enough food stores to feed four of my columns for an entire seasonal round and beyond. You number barely fourteen in total, and the only thing that gets regularly exercised is your stomachs."

The bishop's eyes widened and his mouth dropped open at the comment, but he said nothing.

"Indeed," Waldon jumped in. "'Tell me, my good Bishop: When *was* the last time you left our fair city to minister to your flock?"

"Well . . . I . . . I have duties! I can't be everywhere at once. If I were to be roaming about the hamlets and border towns, I would not be able serve his lordship's best interests."

Waldon rolled his eyes. "Oh, of course not, Bish—"

"Enough!" Trabonus snapped. "The church stores shall donate 10 percent of their seasonal holdings to the military." Trabonus looked at Hitex. "Can't have our fighting troops going hungry when there is work to be done, can we? Now . . . my navy." He cut his eyes at his brother again. "When shall I see our ships in harbor on the northwest wall?"

"You must remember, my lord," Waldon said, "we are not anywhere near the west coast. It's a long way to the ocean. The repairs to the existing infrastructure are holding well, following the damage that the Scarzen saboteurs caused. But it takes time to widen a water course and deepen its flow enough for the kind of vessel you envisage for exploring."

Now Waldon stood and leaned forward, pointing to the map of Flaxor and it borders, sitting in the middle of the table. "Even though we have used the common channel on our western border all the way to the ocean, we still face many months of digging. Engineering solutions around the natural obstructions are costly in both time and resources. Celeron scouts observe every league we progress. We may have made a joint venture for our mutual benefit, but their patience wanes. Our restriction of their freshwater supply—using arguments of needing lower-water levels for the digging—will not hold indefinitely."

"Well, give them something to chew on," Trabonus said. "Make it clear. They can have clink and prosperous trade—or war. Their choice."

Hitex leaned forward in his chair. "Don't forget," he said, "while their army may not match our numbers, the combined force of their battle mages and troops is formidable."

"And," Blackly said, "don't forget the demon race has been seen in parley with them. I've seen it myself when I was in Bon City. Not an ideal situation to have both turn rogue at same time." As he finished saying it, Blackly felt the weight of Hitex's gaze upon him.

Waldon sat back down and gave a curt nod. "On this we agree, Blackly. War would cripple us logistically on the west front, and with the Scarzen constantly pressing from the south, we'd be forced to defend two borders at the same time. The Scarzen will be back, we *all* know that."

Blackly, though, had now turned his eyes to Hitex, who had not ceased staring at him. "Do you have a question for me, Colonel?"

"I'm just wondering what has taken you into the south again. By the sprig of that lint bush on your right sleeve, you've had the courage to go quite a way into Scarzen territories. What is such reconnaissance for, I wonder?"

Blackly gave Trabonus a glance for instruction on how to proceed. Trabonus offered the slightest shake of his head, and so Blackly removed the telltale piece of debris from his jacket sleeve, then faced Hitex again.

"What, you think you are the only one with field agents garnering intelligence, Colonel?" Blackly asked. "I too have a responsibility to my agents who go far and wide to see to our borders' security. I happened to run across a column of your light horse not far from Yorr Pass."

Colonel Hitex stiffened enough to show that the extent of Blackly's excursions came as a surprise.

"So I was just wondering too, as it happens," Blackly said, then gave a small smile. "Why does the colonel need to be conducting clandestine investigations within Weirawind's walls—without the assistance of the RHS?"

"Firstly I have nothing to report," replied Hitex bluntly. "Secondly, Mr. Blackly, my officers, unlike your cluster of sneak-abouts, operate using Flaxon military's strict ethical standards, both on and off the battlefield." Hitex looked to Trabonus. "My lord, when I have something to report, you shall have it immediately. I'm concealing nothing." Hitex noted Trabonus eyeing him carefully and sighed. "In recent days one of my patrols discovered signs of camp activity not our own near the old northeast wall.

"And who was it?" Trabonus asked.

"It appeared to have been a small Scarzen encampment hurriedly vacated. They must have been taken by surprise, as we rarely find any evidence of them settling in anywhere. I had considered it may be linked with the recent sabotage of the dam, and intended to alert Magistrate Waldon of the find after this meeting."

"Hmm," Waldon said. "Has it anything to do with our ambushed border patrols of late?"

"That is the other possibility," Hitex said. "As the good magistrate knows, a recent covert meeting was set up in the Yorr Fields neutral zone. We had received a letter of truce from the Scarzen, something unheard of previously. It was a request for parley. They asserted a way forward had to be found to stop the guerilla war on our mutual border. The letter asked for a meeting between a small party of my trusted command and a small representative unit from Scarza."

Waldon reached into his satchel for another piece of parchment. "Yes," he said, reading from the document, "a Scarzen noble called . . . Titarliaa."

"A Scarzen noble!" Trabonus thumped the table. "Waldon, you go too far. I sanctioned no such thing. You have this demon in custody, I take it?"

"Ah, no, my lord, I do not. That was not the point of the exercise. And, no, you didn't sanction this standard military investigation to gain possible advantage over our lifelong enemy. You were off on a hunting trip with the Chou Dynasty representative in the east. I understand you made first contact with another offering from their king's courtesan court—the Princess Mei Hua, wasn't it?"

Trabonus drew back and furrowed his brow. "What has that to do with the price of chickens?

Waldon gave a weak shrug. "You sanctioned my governance of the borders on the day of your ascension to regency, and therefore this request for a meeting fell under my jurisdiction—Article 9 of the Flaxon Charter of Land Defense, if you recall. Thus, in the regent's absence, I was obligated to act once said information came to light. To not have done so would have seen me in breach of my duty as Flaxor's high magistrate."

Trabonus knew he had no credible counter to his brother's superior knowledge of the law. He licked his thin lips, contemplating a response.

"See it through," came a faint whisper from behind the regent's ear. *"Let him have his game."*

"Why would you even consider such a parley?" Trabonus asked. "My standing orders are to have every Scarzen's head on a javelin and displayed on our common border."

"A law we vigilantly attempt to uphold, my lord," Hitex said. "But a tall order to be accomplished against the likes of the Scarzen. It has proven hard to do over the last two Flaxon generations despite our most determined efforts. Unless we have them at a distance on open ground, with overwhelming onager and cross-bolt coverage, their battle circles, stature, and sheer agility dominate the field."

"Yet several times you've achieved decisive victories in seasons past," Waldon offered in support.

"Yes, but only at the cost of great numbers to do so," Hitex said. "Numbers that are not sustainable in a protracted war."

Waldon sighed and faced his brother. *"I* sanctioned the parley, yes. I believed the intelligence gleaned from such a meeting would expose that a plot designed to weaken Flaxor's defenses was in play. I believe that even more firmly now. I believe the Scarzen to be instruments of destruction."

"Really? How so?" Trabonus asked.

"I will say first that many of your loyal troops sacrificed their lives to uncover the truth," Waldon said.

"That is what troops are for," Trabonus said.

Thankfully Hitex ignored the heartless comment.

Waldon leaned forward to speak. "We found evidence that the Chou intend on pitting us against the Scarzen in open war. Once both sides are sufficiently weakened, the Chou then mean to sweep in to take both Flaxor and Scarza in a single bold move."

Somewhat surprised at the Chou's audacity, Trabonus just sat in his chair, thinking through what had just been reported.

"Hmmm," Blackly said. "As a matter of fact, I heard a whisper that the expressions of love by Princess Mei Hua were naught but a ploy on the Chou king's part. My information said that he planned to have you kidnapped, my lord—something I could not prove or dismiss . . . until now. My informant said that the stubbing of your toe in camp and subsequent early departure saw their opportunity undone. This would seem to corroborate the information just now laid bare here."

Waldon rolled his eyes again and said, "So, Blackly, back to the letter. I smelled the guile of the Chou. The note said the Scarzen wished to parley over water issues near the south neutral zone."

"Anything involving the Scarzen is a deception," Trabonus said.

"Correct," Waldon said, nodding. "But not when it comes to battlefield honor and the giving of their word as warriors."

"Agreed," Hitex said. "This has been proven at every turn that my officers and I have experienced in my fifty full seasons as head of military. The Scarzen say what they mean in such arrangements, and if everyone sticks to the agreement, parties separate without bloodshed—to kill or be killed on another day."

"What's your point?" Trabonus asked.

Waldon reached for his satchel and held it in his hands at the ready. "Certain terms used in the common tongue of the note are never used by the Scarzen in parley," he said. "But the Chou, who have had far fewer dealings with the

Scarzen than we, would not know that. Scarzen use of common tongue script is impatient and direct."

Waldon now produced two bloodstained parchment notes and laid them on the table. "The note to us is styled with the guile of a royal court. Not like a Scarzen communication at all. A Scarzen hand in common tongue is forceful. The words are almost scratches, just like that unintelligible scrawl they used in the note we intercepted on its way to the Celeron."

"Still have trouble decipherin' it," Blackly cut in.

"Look here at the structure," said Waldon, pointing at one parchment. "It is far too refined. And then this note we apparently sent them bearing your signature . . . It is consistent with our way of communicating, but there is one major flaw."

"Which is?" Trabonus asked.

"You didn't write or send such a note, my lord."

"I see," said Trabonus, hand cupping his chin. "So a meeting took place, then?"

"It did," Hitex said. "As you can see, both notes describe a maximum of three per side to attend. My officer, Major Bollard, disregarded the note's orders and took almost a full company, likely intending an ambush. Very foolish since the Yorr Fields neutral zone is the perfect combat ground for the Scarzen."

"And what happened?" Trabonus asked.

Waldon looked to each of the Flaxon at the table, then back at his brother. "We did not carry the day well. When nothing was heard from Major Bollard for some time, I sent a patrol to find out what happened. It seems a massacre of our side ensued after the Scarzen reacted to an ambush and what must have been seen as a breaking of the agreement. As we've discussed, they are sticklers for such protocol."

"And?" Trabonus said.

"Dead to the last soldier, I'm afraid," Waldon said. "There was some evidence of Quall involvement too. Small footprints were found next to the body of a very large Scarzen who'd met their match at close quarters."

Blackly shook his head and stared into nothingness as he muttered, "Nasty little devils, those bloody Quall." He placed a couple fingers on a nasty scar on his right cheek, remembering his own painful experience.

"We also recovered some Quall arrows," Waldon said. "And two signature throwing blades as added proof of their involvement. The blades are unique to the clan of Black Mountain. Whom they were working for can't be determined, as happens in most cases with the Quall."

Turning a bit, Waldon gave a sharp glance to his brother. "They must have left in a hurry. They are rarely that careless."

"Quall!" the bishop nearly spat. "Wretched vermin—bile of the evil one."

"To be sure, Your Grace," Hitex said. "However, I seem to recall the church too has seen the need for their services from time to time. Situations requiring plausible deniability when an infidel is identified, no?"

The bishop shuffled in his seat and cleared his throat. "Well. One must fight fire with fire to protect our fragile masses."

Ignoring the verbal sparring, Trabonus asked, "Why couldn't the Scarzen have employed the Quall? They are both as abhorrent as each other."

Hitex shook his head. "As I've mentioned, Scarzen have an honor code and do their *own* killing. The use of Quall to do a Scarzen's work would be beneath them, particularly in something as disdainful as a double-cross in open parley. Just because Scarzen are twice as tall as us and have features akin to chiseled stone, it does not mean they are dullards. My scout found Scarzen boot prints that indicated a very small party, no more than three—per the agreement. After the skirmish they were the only boot prints leading away . . . south."

Waldon gave a heavy sigh. "Three versus thirty for a total loss of the greater number is embarrassing."

"Unacceptable is what it is!" Trabonus said.

"It is the mark of their prowess on the battlefield," Hitex said. "Something we as soldiers must learn from and respect—or be prepared to take huge losses time and again."

Trabonus waved the comment off and asked, "What did you ultimately hope to achieve with your battlefield play, Colonel?"

"An enemy of my enemy can at times be made my ally, and put to good use," Hitex said.

Blackly snorted a laugh, then asked, "Is that from Hitex's *Battlefield Manual of 'What the frick do we do now when our ass is handed to us'*?"

Hitex glared at him. "No, Blackly. It's from Hitex's observation of victors and vanquished in war. Learn from your enemy's victories, Blackly, or die wishing you had. Surely the esteemed spymaster understands such basics of war." Hitex looked back to the regent. "Once the magistrate and I learned what the Chou had attempted to do, my aim was to have the Scarzen focus turned on a common enemy—a move that would hopefully provide a crippling blow to the Chou without the loss of one Flaxon soldier."

"Oh, that's very calculating, Colonel," the bishop said.

"Yes, it was. Such a coup would have forced the Chou king to commit his forces and logistics elsewhere, allowing for a sound offensive to be mounted in the east. Victory in hand, we would then march on the Chou capital of Da Loong. The subsequent siege would see them sue for peace in a matter of a few short moons. In this way we would keep both the Chou and Celeron in their place."

Trabonus, the bishop, and Blackly exchanged glances, impressed by the audacity of Hitex's plan. It came as no surprise to Waldon, however, who just sat there grinning smugly. He knew his friend's capability well enough.

"Whether the Quall were paid by the Chou to assassinate officers on both sides to incite war from the shadows will never be known," Waldon said. "It fits with usual Chou methodology in my mind, however. One thing is sure: the Scarzen trust us less now than ever. Major Bollard's actions sent the message to the Scarzen command that our leaders are unscrupulous and impulsive. They will use that. I would."

Trabonus sat back in his seat, blowing a breath through his lips with a harsh flutter. "Well, this is an unexpected turn of events," he said. "I think it's time to take a moment to ponder this. We shall break and return to conclude shortly."

All nodded in agreement and stood to stretch their legs. After pouring some wine, Waldon joined Hitex by the center windows. The latched outside shutters lightly tapped the window frames, buffeted by the gale. A focused conversation began between the two that didn't go unnoticed by Blackly, who'd kept to himself while sipping on a mug of char near the hearth. Trabonus and the bishop, meanwhile, had moved to the other side of the hearth in clandestine conversation of their own.

CHAPTER

2

Unsuspecting Madness

"I told you, Waldon is up to something," the bishop said in a low voice. He eyed the regent and then looked at the flaming hearth. "He and Hitex collude against you often. They don't respect you. I think Waldon is digging for further evidence in your father's death. Is the Quall elder still alive?"

"Well, yes, of course he is," Trabonus said. "Waldon must have discovered the other Quall somehow and then paid them off for information, intending to turn the tide in his favor."

"You mean the one *you* hired to compromise your father's longevity?"

"We must find that Quall," said Trabonus, "and have it silenced."

"If Waldon has discovered through them your involvement in your father's departure, and *my* connection therein, things could get out of hand for all of us very quickly. Do you think he knows?"

Trabonus's expression turned grim. "Not in the least. Careful, Magnus. Stay the course and keep your word. If I go down, you'll be in front helping to soften the fall."

Just then, Blackly sidled up in his well-practiced way. "Excuse me, sir," he said softly. "Sorry to interrupt. I thought you should know, there's been more whispers of the two spies we've been trackin' inside the city. 'Specially that one who's always with the gray dog.'"

"What is he talking about?" the bishop asked, looking at Trabonus.

The regent glanced at Magnus with a small hint of a blush and took a moment to think. "Oh, just another archaic text contesting the Maker's Law."

"I've been trying to track it down ahead of the Celeron, sir," Blackly said. "They've put a hefty price on its acquisition." He smiled.

"Thought I might make a killing, if you know what I mean," Trabonus said, nodding to the bishop.

"Back to the spies, sir," Blackly said. "I caught wind that one of them was seen in the tavern near the south gates. One of my boys followed him from the tavern across the south quarter. Lost him after he entered a stable."

"Lost the spy?" asked the bishop.

"No, Your Grace, lost *my* man. Strange thing was, 'brown coat and hat' was all my man said to the stable hand who'd found him before he died. Had a forceful dagger puncture wound to his back and three in his gut. But, sir, the wounds were black and turned to stone. It's the likes of which I've never seen."

"What!" the bishop blurted out.

Hitex and Waldon broke their own whispers and looked their way.

Noticing the unwanted attention, Blackly turned to the servery. "Perhaps some char will help to settle that gut pain, Your Grace."

As Magnus gave a nod, Blackly poured a mug of the chocolate-colored liquid and handed it to him. Waldon and Hitex went back to their conversation.

Blackly leant in to whisper, "Poison blade, I expect, sir. Don't know whether my lad was runnin' or chasin'. The wounds could have occurred either way.

That's the second one of mine in as many weeks who tried to chase down the same mark and paid for it with his life."

"What of the other spy you mentioned?" Trabonus asked.

"Well, that's the thing, sir. The first mark—the one in the brown coat and hat—he was at the tavern last night askin' about any newly arrived couriers for the regent."

"Was he now?" Trabonus said.

"Yes, sir. Said he was workin' for us—uh . . . you, sir. The courier was mine to meet that night, and the tavern owner knew it. Courier was bringing me this."

From a pocket inside his coat Blackly withdrew a small brown leather cylinder and handed it to Trabonus.

"This's the one you've been waiting for, sir. Same markin's. It was taken from a dead Grizzly scout outside of Gantry."

"You mean a Scarzen?" Magnus asked.

"Yes, Your Grace. No sign of a big skirmish, and only one other set of boot prints. Saw the boot marks myself. That's where I've been. Not a toe bigger than mine, and no mistake, sir. That big bull was killed alone just like the others we found inside the city. Knife wounds black and turned to stone just like them. Seems we have killer of considerable power in our midst, sir."

"Hex protect us," Magnus said, glancing skyward.

"Who among any of our cultures can be strong enough to best a Scarzen one on one?" Trabonus mused aloud. "If a demon like that could be turned to one's employ, then . . ."

Trabonus faded off into an internal trail of thought while holding the sealed scroll. *Impressive . . . Someone prepared to take on a Scarzen?*

Blinking himself back to the moment at hand, Trabonus said, "Go on, Blackly."

"Amongst his inquiries, the fella in the brown coat and hat asked the tavern owner if anyone has seen the man who's always with a little gray dog. That's how I know the two are related and are workin' together. The tavern owner told me he hadn't seen the man in question, and told the fella so. He remarked also that the one in the brown coat made his blood run cold."

"Is he a threat to us?" asked the bishop.

If they give 'im half a chance and all of it painful, thought Blackly, but only gave a shrug.

Trabonus and the bishop stared at Blackly, waiting for further comment.

"Anyway, the fella in the brown coat then leaves the tavern—and I miss him by a snap of fingers, but I was able to at least collect your mail. So then I leave. And, Maker's grace, who should walk through the door a sneeze after my departure? None other than the second spy in question, the barkeep tells me. Our spy walks in with his dog, on no tether." Blackly leant in again. "This time he's dressed in Flaxon uniform, all pips and lanyard. He's purporting to be a major in Hitex's own regiment."

Conversation stalled as Hitex approached the char table to pour himself a cup. They each gave one another their best false smile, and the colonel then moved back to rejoin Waldon in conversation.

"A Celeron subversive, I wager, sir," Blackly went on. "Sneaky bastards, them. He inquired about the one in the brown coat. The tavern owner reported to me that he then saw the officer and his dog leave by the back alley after he told them the brown coat just went out the front. Very strange."

"Yes . . . it is," Trabonus said.

"Can we identify which company the spy is masquerading as an officer in?" the bishop asked.

"Workin' on that, Your Grace. The tavern owner sent a lad to follow the stranger and his dog. But the tail said he lost them in a blind alley in the east quarter with no way out or some such rubbish. They just vanished, he swore on his mother's grave."

"Hmm. If there is a thread connecting my brother to any of this, I want to know immediately," Trabonus said, looking across to Waldon. "You've done well, Blackly. Leave us now."

Blackly retreated to his chair at the table. At the hearth Trabonus carefully broke the wax seal of the cylinder. From it he withdrew the contents, consisting of an aged page from a book. He unrolled the first couple of inches of the parchment and examined it with interest. The revealed line of the Scarzen Chicaa script made Trabonus smile.

Yes . . . appears to be exactly what I was hoping for.

The bishop leaned closer to see. "Maker, keep us safe!" he whispered.

"Yes, Magnus. Another page of the *Tome of Zharkaa* for you to solve."

"I must tell you, my lord, I'm increasingly uncomfortable with what I've seen come from the few pages we already have. Even the individual leaves have power of their own. This is a dangerous game, my lord. There is something hidden on the pages—I felt a dark hand clutch my soul the last time. It was omnipotent but malevolent. If the others find out I've been translating Scarzen heretical text for you, I will be cast out."

Trabonus heard the panic growing in the bishop's voice, and he slid the parchment into a gambeson pocket.

"And you will be called to the inquisition," Magnus said. "Hex will be most displeased."

Trabonus's expression hardened. "Stop prattling. You worry too much, Magnus. Hex is in my corner, remember? Your own scrying pool said as much. We are closer than ever to success."

Trabonus glanced at Hitex and Waldon, still immersed in discussion.

"Come with me," the regent said to the bishop.

Then Trabonus led Magnus to a side door, opened it, and led the way inside.

***

The much smaller room they entered served as an annex for Trabonus's main study, through another door off to the right. A large open window framed by heavy vermilion curtains stood to the left. To the right a fireplace still burned from earlier activities. Shadows of the hanging hearth tools danced on the fringe of the firelight that partially illuminated the bookcase standing adjacent.

The bishop pressed the door shut and locked it. He then turned to Trabonus with a concerned expression.

"Come in and steady yourself, Bishop," Trabonus said. "You look a trifle ruffled."

"Ruffled! A murdered Scarzen brought down by someone wielding a blade found in a neutral zone settlement—out in the open. We both know who's done this. Does this not bother you?"

"Not at all," Trabonus said. "Why should it?"

"Well, to start with, it takes ten of our best light horse to bring down one isolated Scarzen. How hard do you think it will be to control the same individual who can singlehandedly eliminate one with nothing but a long knife?"

Trabonus shrugged. "Clink, a great deal of leverage, finesse, and superior intellect. There are any number of tools to ensure I have the upper hand."

"My lord, it happened in Gantry Town! In the name of the Maker, it's the biggest haven of secrets and whisper trading in Ludd. What was Starlin doing there anyway? What reason could he have?"

"I don't know—not my concern."

"Loose tongues in Gantry Town could easily point this mischief in our direction. The dead Scarzen was found carrying Flaxon articles. Our mysterious brown-coated friend—the very same one we've been colluding with —was seen standing over the body at the scene. My sources say several deaths with his signature marker—the same marker as the ones Blackly mentioned found here—were discovered there."

Trabonus waved a dismissive hand. "He's simply cleaning up the loose ends, Magnus."

The bishop grunted. "How does bumping off a nine-foot-tall Scarzen warrior in the middle of Gantry Town neutral settlement with witnesses looking on *tie up loose ends?*"

"I have no idea why Starlin had to deal with the Scarzen in such a public place, Magnus. I'm sure he had his reasons. Be happy another one is dead. None of it connects me to Father's death if that's your concern."

"There is still the question of our Quall assassin you can't find, and there's still whatever Waldon is holding over you! He does have something, doesn't he?"

Now Trabonus shifted his posture, obviously uneasy at the bishop's comment.

Magnus nodded. "Yes, I too have eyes and ears in the streets, my lord. Two witnesses saw your last ordered executions happen. Then they turned up dead too. How many more, Trabonus? I knew this would all go bad the moment you committed us both to the cover-up of your father's demise. Waldon is no fool. He'll find out what you've done."

Trabonus gritted his teeth, increasingly angered at the bishop's remarks. "Not if you keep your mouth shut."

"He is as ruthless, methodical, and patient as you are when it comes to getting his way, Trabonus. He's planning something—I know it. I don't want to be in his way when he takes action."

Trabonus frowned. "'When he takes action . . .'? You know, Magnus, your doubt in my ability to handle these matters—I find it disturbing."

"Starlin is no friend, my lord. I tell you, he has a dark agenda of his own in this."

"Possibly. I helped him with some mutually beneficial information."

"What! What kind of information?"

"Careful, Magnus, your power of inquiry only extends so far. Starlin agreed to do a little cleaning up and locate some of the pages I've been looking for. It was a fair trade."

The bishop stared at Trabonus for a long moment, then said, "I have met some evil ones in my time, but Starlin stands on a high mark of his own. I'd rather negotiate with a company of Scarzen than be left vulnerable to him. How did he know about such a closely guarded secret as the pages—tell me that? I've spoken of it to no one. He is not Flaxon born, nor can any of my spies find any news or record of him in lands afar. We know nothing of his background, or how he manages to slip in and out of the city unseen. I've had him followed several times. He always seems to just vanish after turning a corner or passing beyond a door."

Trabonus slit his eyes at Magnus. "I said, I'm handling it! Just keep your mouth shut and stay out of Waldon's way. I'll deal with everything in due course. What's a dead Scarzen or two matter? It can only help our cause. You should be pleased."

"We only agreed on one necessary court elimination! I warned you about Starlin the first time he showed up out of nowhere. I said it wouldn't end there and it hasn't. Now it seems he's picking marks of his own and leaving incriminating evidence that points our way."

"Nonsense. You're a fool, Magnus . . . always hiding behind the skirt of the church the moment one of your schemes runs askew. We had nothing to do with those events. They are separate things. No blame can be laid on me."

The bishop stepped forward. "Trabonus. This is not a time to be dismissive. We could have the entire southern demon horde on our doorstep in force. With such loose play we will end up in an inquisition from inside our walls. If the Scarzen connect the deaths of their scouts and the missing pages of their tome to us, the consequences will be catastrophic."

"*Weakness,*" Trabonus heard in that same whispered voice from behind his ear. "*Fix this—now.*"

"Hiring the Quall to deal with your father was risky enough," pressed the bishop in a forced whisper. "But engaging this Starlin—it's a . . . it's a great step toward madness. His rogue actions will bring our whole bright future down on our heads."

Trabonus nodded as if suggesting agreement. He moved toward a small table opposite the fireside, where several rolled parchment leaves sat in a stack. Then he reached into a pocket and withdrew the parchment that Blackly had just delivered to him, tapping it gently in the palm of his hand, thinking.

"My 'loose play,' as you put, it is bearing fruit, is it not?" Trabonus asked. "Hex seems pleased—nay, even encouraging by all the signs. You've said so yourself. Let me remind you, *Your Grace:* it was *you* who hired the Quall assassin to have my father removed using the sleeping sickness; it was by *your* proxy the services of the assassin guild of Black Mountain were sought."

"Yes, but—"

"Your signature along with mine is on that parchment giving thanks."

"Yes, but I only——"

"You hurt me with your betrayal, Magnus. I am cut deep."

"Betrayal! I never——"

"I have the Quall elder," Trabonus said. "He is now in a secure place and will testify that it was *you* who were the driving force behind my father's sad demise. And it was *you* who used *my* ring seal without me present. Capital offense, that." Trabonus pointed a finger at Magnus. "Ensure you keep your end of the bargain, Your Grace. Hitex and my scheming brother all head in directions that please me, for now. I want to keep it that way. Let them experiment with their plans of modernization and the new black powder, artillery . . . anything that keeps them occupied."

With the realization of how Trabonus had manipulated everything, Magnus stood there, growing paler by the moment. He knew not what to do or say next.

Trabonus smiled. "Hitex's idea to weaponize the Celeron black powder has proven a true strength. It has helped us show the Scarzen we are not to be trifled with." Trabonus shook the rolled parchment under the bishop's nose. "You'll work swiftly to translate the remaining meaning on this next page. Then Hex the Just will be so much closer to resurrection and my end goal. After his resurrection he will name *me* ruler of everything under his skies in appreciation for my services. The *Tome of Zharkaa* states it so, doesn't it?"

"Well, yes, but there is a price."

Trabonus ignored the warning. "Then, Magnus, then all our enemies will be enslaved and pay dearly. They will do my bidding."

"Yes, pay dearly," whispered the voice to him.

Mouth hanging open, aghast at what was just said, the bishop placed a hand on his brow. In despair he looked into Trabonus's cold gray eyes.

"How did we get here?" Magnus asked. *It's as if he's been processed,* the bishop thought, then said, "My lord, I admit I thought in the beginning something could be made of all this to our advantage. But this Starlin . . . he has twisted your point of view with his unsubstantiated claims and knowledge of the translations. How can he know such detail of their real meaning without being in league with the Scarzen scourge? It is Starlin who betrays you, my lord, not I. Double meanings and constant warnings are rife. Have I not made this clear?"

The regent gave a small nod. "Many times."

"Hex the Just and Hex the Dark … they function as one. That union must not be taken for granted. Can you not recognize the strangeness with which the pages fell into your possession shortly after Starlin arrived? Each page has only come via death and suffering, with Starlin very close behind."

"This bothers you how, Your Grace? It's never bothered you before. It is a method I've watched you Flaxon clergy of the One God employ with zeal all my life, as it suits you. Why shouldn't I do the same, hm?"

"No, Trabonus. Please! These happenings are not the mark of Hex the Just. The rule of Hex is clear; he is a mirror of the soul. Good action attracts good boons. That is the teaching. Bad ones, well . . ." Magnus hesitated. "You get the idea. Every consequence is manifested through free will and attracts an equal reaction. Nothing created, nothing destroyed—through Hex everything exists. The last translations of the tome's pages say that Hex the Dark means to purge this world of all debts owed. This mean's *all* of Flaxor, including *you,* my lord." Magnus swallowed, nervously waiting for a reply.

"Then you're in luck, Magnus, because you yourself said my name— *Trabonus*—translates as *Redeemer* according to the pages of the tome." Trabonus touched the bishop on the shoulder. "I was born to aim highest, Magnus, and that can't come without a little rough ground."

The bishop felt at a loss for words. On the writing table behind Trabonus, Magnus noticed the weathered leather-bound spine of a large book. Partially covered with gray cloth, it piqued his interest because of its appearance. He frowned, remembering a description of the *Tome of Zharkaa* that Starlin had referred to once, and so he moved to step toward it for a closer look.

"I've only seen but a few pages," Magnus said. "Is that . . . ?"

Trabonus glanced at the tome and softly stepped to block the view, forcing Magnus to stop.

"How can that be?" Magnus asked, looking at Trabonus. "We did not know it truly existed at all until a moon ago. That's when the first torn page blew in through your bedchamber window. Don't you remember? That was also when Starlin first appeared to explain its significance and the book it belonged to." Magnus's eyes widened. "It was Starlin, wasn't it? He brought you the body of the tome, didn't he? Why have you said nothing?"

"I don't need to explain myself to you, Bishop. It is mine to use as I see fit."

"My lord. Please! The further I translate the tome's pages, the more the text points to a labyrinth of insidious entanglement. It is evil. I've told you, the first half of the translation I've been able to make clear is from a section called 'Transmutation of Souls.' It stands in direct contradiction to the explanation Starlin gave. Just from seeing the top line on the page Blackly gave you a few moments ago, I can tell that this is *not* a path to enlightenment with Hex. The invocation in the passage will actually instruct someone how to irreversibly exchange one life's destiny for another."

Trabonus offered a small smile. "Excellent. Just what I need: a chance to assume the position I was rightfully born to hold. Nothing will bind me to this carcass of existence, Magnus—nothing."

With wide eyes the bishop shook his head. "No, my lord, you don't understand. There is a deception in play. I'm sure of it. Trabonus, I'm your friend. I do what I do in your best interests. But we have gone too far. Could we not take time to think the matter through? Yes, I initially agreed with Starlin's claim that your name meant *Redeemer*, based on my first look at the pages. But my independent translation of your name with all of the pages I now have in hand—plus what I saw of the newest page—leads me to believe your name rather means *Reaper of the Many . . .* or *Soul Eater.*"

"What? What are you carrying on about?"

"I needed to be sure, and now I am. With what I've just seen, Starlin's assertion that you will be the *Redeemer of the Many,* or the *Emancipator,* is completely twisted."

Trabonus folded his arms and offered only a steely gaze.

"Look," Magnus said. "That first page translated states, 'Truth is shaped by the free will of the agent. One must trust the signs to know the truth.' But what signs? We don't know enough about the translation to be sure. And with what I have just seen, the translation errs much more toward the former evil than the latter benevolent outcome."

Just then, from the corner of his eye, Magnus thought he saw the sinister figure of Starlin sitting in the open window frame. He shot an agitated look in that direction to check, but the view only showed an empty open window and the stormy night sky beyond.

"What's wrong with you now, Magnus?" Trabonus asked. "You look as if you've seen a ghost. Seriously, you're becoming more paranoid by the moment."

The bishop snapped his view back to Trabonus, covering his mouth with a horrified realization. "Heart of Hex! Trabonus, no, this is . . . this is . . . What have I done?"

The whisper of a nasty mocking chuckle met their ears from the background. Trabonus only smiled upon hearing it, but the bishop's eyes grew even wider. The tension in the room spiked.

"Whatever do you mean, Magnus? You look pale. Do you need to sit down?"

"You said our actions would keep the Scarzen scourge at bay—make our streets *safer*!" Magnus said his last words through chattering teeth. "It hasn't! Instead there's been murder in our streets, and now their demon ways have crept insidious inside our city walls. All while we did nothing!" Now Magnus steadied himself and glared at the regent. "*You've* allowed this evil, this Starlin, to dance amongst us with impunity! It is reckless and to the detriment of us all."

Trabonus's expression hardened. "How dare you!"

Magnus shook his head, his jaw set. "The church must now intervene," he said. "You have been bewitched by this cad. His twisted words only say what you want to hear. To protect you, and our fair Flaxor, as head of the church and archdiocese, I invoke Law 47 of the Flaxon Charter. In the name of Hex and the citizens of Flaxor, you are relieved of office until clear resolution of this matter can be found. I—" Magnus cut his monologue short upon seeing the burning hatred in Trabonus's eyes.

"You can't be serious, priest! You actually think . . . You really think you can pull rank by using that old Special Exceptions Law!" Arms by his sides, Trabonus tightened his fingers into white-knuckled fists. "You think to declare me—ME—Trabonus, regent of Flaxor, addle-minded? Why, you . . . you charlatan! You won't seize power over ME!"

Being taller than Trabonus, Magnus now straightened up to further bolster his courage to counter his regent. "A temporary cessation of your controlling wisdom is all, my lord. We must ensure the good citizens of Flaxor are not betrayed by the insidious behaviors of an unsound mind. The royal church physician will determine the extent of any derangement or beguilement foisted on you by a subversive, such as Starlin."

"Really!"

"It is in your best interest, my lord. If you refuse this small imposition, I will translate the demon texts no longer. Without my skill to guide the translation, your understanding of the *Tome of Zharkaa* is rudimentary at best. Seeking a way forward without my aid will lead to catastrophe without the smallest doubt."

Trabonus shuffled in anger. The bishop stepped closer to drive his point home.

"Many pages are still missing. One misinterpretation, one poorly pronounced word, my lord, and you'll just as easily invoke Hex's wrath instead of his blessing. Please, stand aside."

"Betrayer," Trabonus heard whispered in his ear.

Magnus watched Trabonus take a steady breath and then saw him seemingly relax—or was it something else?

"He mocks you," came the whispered voice.

The howl of the wind outside increased and coals crackled loudly in the hearth before a clutch of burning embers spat forward onto the stone floor. Both the bishop and Trabonus were prompted to step wide, with the bishop ending up closer to the table. Trabonus watched the bishop focus again on the partially covered tome. Magnus reach out and pulled the cloth away, exposing the tome fully. On the front cover, clear for all to see, was a Scarzen heraldic symbol unknown to Magnus: two eyes on a circle divided, embossed deeply into the travel-worn leather.

"The tome—and nearly complete?" the bishop said just above a whisper. "How—When?" He shook his head. "This must be taken into church custody," Magnus said, reaching for the tome.

"Leave that be!" Trabonus said with a snarl.

A gust of wind struck the shutters from outside and then blew them closed with a slap, as if heavy hands wanted them sealed in.

"Deal with him," came a hateful voice from behind Trabonus—and the bishop also heard it clearly.

Magnus gasped and looked around the room, but there was no one to be seen.

"By Hex's name, you are cursed," the bishop said, now seizing the tome. "You give me no alternative. This must be destroyed!"

Wind hit the shutters hard, accompanied by a howl as if a great evil was trying to force its way in.

"YOU WILL NOT!" Trabonus shouted.

The bishop ignored him and turned toward the fire, holding the tome high overhead in both hands. "This ends now!" Magnus yelled.

"You fool—NO!"

Trabonus rushed forward and shoved the bishop hard. Magnus fell in an uncontrolled sprawl. His face made a sharp smack as it struck the grainy stone surface of the hearth, breaking his nose. The tome left his grip and flew to the floor. The symbol glinted in the firelight as it skittered across the floor toward Trabonus.

"Ahh! Ahhh, I'm bleeding," the bishop whimpered, trying to push himself up into a sitting position.

Trabonus glared at Magnus, insane with rage.

"Now!" snapped that same hateful voice to Trabonus. *"End him!"*

Slowly Trabonus bent down and retrieved the book as the bishop raised himself to his knees, groggy from his fall, with blood streaming from his nose. They both heard the sudden sound of the others approaching, along with murmured voices. Trabonus paid the door a single glance before all his attention fell back on the bishop.

"You want this, you demented old fool? Then I'll give it to you!"

Trabonus gripped the tome with both hands, teeth clenched. As Magnus turned to look at him, face bloody, Trabonus swung the tome at his head, striking the bishop a vicious blow. The force of his first action knocked Magnus senseless, driving him facedown onto the edge of the hearth. His forehead struck the corner of the step in front of the hearth, cracking his skull. Trabonus stepped in and pounded Magnus thrice more plus one, the last blow sending him to oblivion. The bishop's blood smeared across the cover of the tome.

"Now you see!" Trabonus shouted at the bleeding corpse. "See what *you've* done!"

Thumping and shouting erupted from the other side of the door.

"My lord!" shouted Blackly. "What's wrong? Are you alright?"

"Open the door!" Waldon demanded.

Ignoring their calls, still in utter fury, Trabonus dropped the tome and slapped a hand on the dead bishop's back and neck. "Tell your case to Hex!"

He heaved the body up and onto the burning coals. As the bishop's garments caught fire and the smell of his burning flesh filled the room, Trabonus picked up the bloodied *Tome of Zharkaa*.

Staring at it, even as those on the other side of the door struggled to gain entry, to the regent's amazement, he saw the wet blood of the bishop being swiftly absorbed. With that, its weathered leather cover shimmered in the firelight, transforming into something pristine—dark, but somehow magnificent. He watched transfixed as the two-dimensional symbol on the cover morphed into something alive.

"Put your back into it, Blackly!" Hitex ordered.

The next charge saw the door almost broken through. A fading whisper drew Trabonus's attention to the tome: *"It is undone. I am corrupted. Blood of an innocent. It is undone."*

Trabonus hurried to conceal the tome back under the cloth on the table and then turned to face the door. A final charge saw the three individuals on the other side spill into the room through the doorway.

"In the Maker's name!" Waldon shouted. "What's happened here?"

Trabonus looked to the covered tome in silence. Then he drew a breath and faced the others, beginning to tear up.

"He was my friend," Trabonus said with his best convincing sob. "Like a father to me. We were discussing the matters just presented. Then, without warning, he became enraged when I said we had to show more temperance for what was occurring on our borders. 'Many lives are at stake,' I told him. He wouldn't listen. He said something in a tongue I failed to understand. It was chilling. Then a strange presence filled the room and began to whisper incantations . . . something dark—evil. I was frightened for my life. It was then I shouted for help. When none came, I panicked."

Trabonus looked to the facedown body of the bishop smoldering on the fire, his bottom lip trembling. "His eyes suddenly turned fire orange." He paused to sob. "Just like the southern demons . . . and then he lashed out at me as if possessed. I was . . . I was honestly terrified." Trabonus took a soft step forward, presenting bloodied open palms. "I tried to push him aside. We struggled for a moment. He fell—there." Trabonus pointed. "You can see the rest."

The other three exchanged stunned glances. They stared at the bishop's blistering body.

Waldon clamped a hand over his nose and mouth. "God, the stench. Smells like he's fouled himself."

Blackly looked a little closer. "I think you might be right, sir."

"For Hex's sake, Blackly!" Hitex said. "Get him out of the fire before anyone else sees him that way."

"Shouldn't I douse the flames first, sir?"

"Just put him out and open a damn window."

Blackly stepped across and grabbed the body by the ankles, then pulled it from the fireplace, still burning. He dropped the bishop's legs and then moved toward the closed window.

"I meant put the *flames* out," Hitex said. He grabbed a bucket in a nearby corner and threw the liquid contents on the flaming body.

The resulting steam made everyone take a step back as a blast of ammonia assaulted their olfactory senses.

"I had intended to use the clean-water bucket here under the window, sir," said Blackly, holding the pail up. "I know our lordship's tinkle may well be blessed, but I thought it more respectful to douse His Eminence with water from the skies."

"I never liked the old stump," said Waldon, waving a hand under his nose, "but I'd never wish that upon him. Maker's name, he stinks."

Waldon moved forward, noting the regent shaking, and helped his brother to a chair.

"How do we deal with this?" asked Hitex. "This death will send the court into panic."

"The church inquisitory will want to claim the body and begin immediate investigation, that's certain," Waldon said.

"That would be bad," Blackly said.

"*Someone* or something will have to answer for the unusual passing," Hitex said.

Blackly tossed a look from Hitex to the body. "Unusual? I'd see this as suspicious if I was head of the investigation."

Waldon stepped forward and nodded. "That's exactly why you will investigate the matter personally, Blackly. And you'll find this sad death to be one that occurred by misadventure."

"Misadventure?"

"He tripped," Waldon said.

"Oh. Yes, sir. I see, sir. Yes, he definitely tripped. Poor old stick fell face-first into the coals and smothercated hisself—terrible business."

"And our regent?" Hitex asked.

Waldon glanced over at his brother and then back to Hitex. "At great personal risk . . . courageously did all he could to save our beloved head of church."

They all looked at the regent, considering how they might carry the façade through.

"Well," Blackly said, "I'll present my findings as you've instructed."

"Yes," said Waldon. "Only add that, *initially,* the bishop was agitated about a private matter and you overheard the bishop request a personal audience with the regent. That you heard through the door our regent pleading with the disturbed bishop to calm down. Then you heard a struggle begin where the regent must have been forced to defend himself. The scuffle resulted with the bishop's demise."

"Good triumphs over evil," said Hitex, nodding. "Hmm, I don't like it, but that should keep the masses happy."

"Brilliant, sir," Blackly said. "The clergy love a good demon story."

"As magistrate my testimony and eyewitness account of events will be weight enough to sway any doubt," Waldon said. He looked at Trabonus and nodded. "Come, brother, let's get you to the greeting room. You need to be prepared for the inquisitors when they arrive. Just play to your strength: manipulate everyone."

"Don't worry about me," Trabonus said. "Just see that you fix this mess."

"Ferdinand," Waldon said to Hitex, "best that you vacate the premises through the hidden door behind us. The passage will take you across to the east wing where you can emerge without drawing attention. Can't have the leader of the military implicated in any way."

"Agreed. So we'll talk of it later," Hitex said, leaving the others to deal with Trabonus and the body.

"Blackly," said Waldon. "See that no one leaves the castle until this is dealt with. Take the body through the secret corridor and place it in the regent's prayer room. Lay him out respectfully there and call for the bishop's aids. Post a guard."

"Yes, Magistrate," Blackly said.

Waldon then escorted Trabonus away, leaving Blackly to clean up.

CHAPTER

3

Dirty Business

It took Blackly a few minutes to tidy up the gruesome scene and then haul the body over to the secret corridor. Struggling with the body into the dimly lit passage that Hitex had used a few moments before, Blackly quickly worked up a sweat. Barely inside the passage he stopped for a breather and then dropped the body unceremoniously with a thud. Wiping his furrowed brow with a dirty handkerchief, he bent again to finish the task.

"Only a short distance now, preacher. You always were a fat old bastard, but I didn't think your old lard-ass was *this* heavy."

"So what nefarious errand did the regent have you on this time, hm?" came Hitex's voice out of the corridor's darkness.

Startled, Blackly dropped the body again and spun sharply, reaching into his pocket for his pacifier. "You shouldn't sneak up on a Flaxon in the dark like that, my old Colonel. Might get yourself very hurt and no mistake."

Hitex glared at him. "You can't intimidate me, Blackly. I've seen zukaa bullshit harder than the Flaxon you are. I've waited here to ask you a question."

"Have you now, Colonel? And what would that be, sir?"

"Again, what reprehensible errand has our illustrious leader got you chasing this time?"

Blackly chuckled. "You know the rules, Colonel. What plays between me and his lordship, stays between me and his lordship. Would be my skin if he thought I was whisperin' out of turn."

The colonel stood firm for a moment, staring Blackly down, then said, "I don't like you, Blackly. I don't like you worth the toe of my boot. You are a cad, a stain upon our fair Flaxor. That you are in the good graces of his lordship is all that keeps you safe. You are tolerated in some circles for the tasks you will perform that others will not."

"You mean like the example I'm cleaning up for all you *fine* gentry now, sir?" Blackly nodded toward the body at his feet.

Hitex unclipped the hilt of his war saber hanging from his belt and took hold of the grip firmly. "If you don't give me something strikingly good right now, Blackly, you'll be marched at sword-point to my military cells for interrogation and wish by Hex's beard that his lordship was skinning you alive."

Blackly took the margin of a breath to consider his options, then shrugged. "His lordship is dealing in some arcane mischief. He says it will put us on top of the food chain and put even the Scarzen scourge under his thumb. He had me collecting pages of their demon scribblings from a source that has knowledge of their lands."

"This source's name?"

"I only know him as Starlin, and he's not one to be trifled with."

"A Celeron?"

Blackly gave a slow shake of his head. "No, sir. His origin is unknown, but one whisper reports he comes from far across the great Shalane Ocean. That's all I know, sir."

When Hitex gave no immediate reply, Blackly tried to read the hard expression on the colonel's face, but he gave little away.

"Tend to your task," Hitex finally said. "I may have questions for you later. You may go."

Blackly heaved the body back into its dragging position and moved on past Hitex.

"Oh, and Blackly."

The dragging stopped, and Blackly looked back over his shoulder.

"Not a word," Hitex said, "to anyone."

"No, sir, not a word."

Hitex waited until Blackly had faded into the shadows of the hallway. He then made his own way out into the streets of Weirawind to walk and think through the night's events.

***

Blackly took care of the body and made the arrangements as ordered. Uneasy about what had unfolded, he thought a quiet tankard of ale and another chat with the tavern owner would help to clear his head. Outside, the dark streets were saturated from the recent downpour. Roof eaves still dribbled from the earlier rain, and the cobblestone streets were strewn with puddles. Blackly gripped the lapels of his gray cold-weather coat to brace against the chill of the breeze pushing its way through the streets. The soft yellow hue of the street oil lamps only offered a vague depth of field for passersby.

As Blackly stepped along, the city's rolling mists made the figures of other citizens appear as silhouettes. All went about their late-night business with deliberate intent to get out of the cold night and indoors. The atmosphere gave the city streets an eerie feel. Nearly two-thirds of the way there, Blackly felt sure he was being followed for a time. Being a master of that game himself, he wanted no eyes on his business tonight. At his next opportunity he ducked down a side alley to shake off his pursuer. Only a few strides in, Blackly stopped dead in his tracks. His intuition told him the place had ambush written all over it. He reached into his inside coat pocket, taking hold of his cosh. Directly in front of him, another figure stepped out from the shadows to bar his way. The individual was backlit by a single lamp a few steps behind.

"Steady there, my lad," Blackly said. "You approach a member of the RHS. Mind your manners now."

The individual said nothing in reply. Blackly focused in on the silhouette. It quickly dawned on him as to who was staring him down. He knew retreat was out of the question. His body filled with apprehension as he stood there, waiting for the shadowy figure to make the next move.

Is he done with me now? Blackly wondered as the hair on his neck stood up.

"Good evening, Blackly. You don't look pleased to see me. Why so worried?" The individual took a couple of paces closer. "Even a shadow crawler like you wouldn't normally use this filthy pathway. Evading anyone in particular?"

Blackly swallowed and took a fraction to shoot a nervous glance over his shoulder to see if retreat was possible. By the time his point of view had returned to the figure addressing him, he'd bridged the gap. Blackly's heart rate surged. The brown-coated individual stood within easy arm's reach. Now clear in the lamplight, the figure's merciless icy stare cut to the core of Blackly's soul.

"Ah . . . Mr. Starlin, sir. It's you. You did give me a start." Blackly cleared his throat and took a tentative step back. "Fancy seein' you out in this sorry part of town on such an unpleasant night."

"I could say the same of you, Blackly. I go where my work takes me," said Starlin in his steady, unnerving manner. "Tonight my works brings me to you."

Blackly swallowed. "Really? Oh, uh, how kind. Why am I bestowed such consideration, sir? Gantry Town is nearly three days' hard ride from here. The last news I received yesterday, it placed you as still being there, sir."

"Did it?"

"I thought I still had time to fulfill your request. You must have rode like Hex's north wind to make your way back so swift."

"You and I have an arrangement, Blackly, do we not?"

"Yes, sir. Indeed we do, sir."

Starlin gave a tight smile. "I did you a considerable favor. Had to go out of my way. Your wife is free of her bone affliction now, isn't she? She shall remain by your side, as agreed, healthy and happy for the rest of your days." Starlin scanned left and then right. "In this forsaken vermin hole, I'd hate to have to reverse your good fortunes."

"I'm forever grateful, sir," said Blackly. "Please don't harm her, sir. She's the one good and pure thing in my stained life. You said so yourself, sir."

Starlin nodded. "I did. And you need to keep that status quo, don't you? So did you do as I instructed?"

"Yes, sir. His lordship received the next page exactly as ordered. But there's been some strife tonight on a couple of fronts."

Starlin's eyebrows went up. "Really? That being?"

"Yes. I'm afraid the bishop, Magnus Targus, took his last breath ahead of your schedule. His lordship and the bishop appear to have had a disagreement, and there was a struggle."

"Oh, that."

Now Blackly furrowed his brow. Starlin's tone suggested he could have witnessed or even provoked the matter himself.

"Anything else?" Starlin asked.

"Uh, yes, sir. That prying Colonel Hitex is poking his nose in again. I thought it was him following me just now. I was on my way to the tavern. He cornered me earlier for information after the bishop's demise. Wanted to know what his lordship had me up to this past while. Threatened to detain me if I didn't give him something solid."

"And what did you give him?"

"I'm sorry, sir, but he pushed me to it!"

"Pushed you to what?"

"He seemed to know more than he was sayin'. I had to give him your name."

Eye's locked on Blackly, Starlin reached casually inside his long brown coat with his right hand. He withdrew a nasty blade—a long stiletto, Blackly recognized. Its four-edged shape, designed for penetrating chainmail, meant that any wound would have great difficulty healing. It appeared a good hand and forearm in length to the hilt, and had a strange crimson glow. Starlin wiped the blade down along his opposite sleeve, which made tiny sparks and a soft sizzling sound as he did it.

"But . . . But . . . I did it as you instructed and no more," Blackly said. "I promise, sir."

Starlin shook his head. "You weren't supposed to take that step until I told you the trap was set. Hope I don't have to teach you a lesson, Blackly. Because I'd be most put out."

With breathtaking speed Starlin lunged with force toward Blackly. He gripped Blackly's coat and the clothing just below his neck. With one powerful hand Starlin slammed Blackly against the stone wall. Starlin raised the blade in his other hand to shoulder height, its deadly tip pointing straight at Blackly's face.

"Did Hitex ask about or say anything about one called Uniss?"

"What? Who? No . . . No, sir."

A realization swept across Starlin's expression. He looked to the entrance of the alley. "You *were* being followed, but it wasn't by me. You need to be more careful, Blackly. There is a lot at stake."

In fear for his life, Blackly raised open hands, shaking his head. Starlin pressed the blade forward. Its tip met the stone wall within a breath of Blackly's cheek. Effortlessly Starlin's blade penetrated the wall up to the hilt, making that same sizzling sound. The stone around the blade's penetration cracked and turned cast-iron gray.

"Follow orders, Blackly. We are nearly there. The one called Uniss normally travels with a short, stocky gray canine. If you find yourself in their company, forfeit your own life rather than tell them anything, or I promise you that your dear Lucania will know unimaginable suffering well beyond this life."

Starlin withdrew his blade and slung Blackly with one hand toward the alley entrance. Blackly fell face-first in a sprawl. Groaning, Blackly pressed himself to a standing position with his back still to Starlin.

"Don't let me down, Blackly."

"I'll not let you down, sir. You have my word."

When Blackly turned, he saw that Starlin had vanished.

***

Stepping along the misty street, Hitex was unaware that only a few short strides ahead, Blackly had just finished his liaison with Starlin. He too had thought to visit a quiet upstairs corner in the same tavern Blackly was heading for. Hands in his coat pockets, Hitex felt full of concern over the events of the last hour.

None of this will go easy. The implications for the Flaxon court are huge. The bishop had the people's favor above Trabonus, if my wife's church circle whisperings are accurate. Easy to see why. Trabonus was a spoilt self-centered prat from the time his mother taught him how to dance. Hitex pursed his lips. *And what is Blackly really up to? Nothing good.*

Here and there oil lamps still illuminated the doorways of some buildings after the squall. To Hitex the surrounding cold, gray features presented as ink lines amidst deeper shadows.

Bitter night for a mind working on troubles to be outdoors.

By the time he'd trudged halfway to his destination, his original interest to be in the company of hard-smoking, card-playing tavern regulars had quickly faded. He stopped at the next cross street to let a horse-drawn pay carriage pass by. He heard some faint murmur of chatting occupants inside. The clip-clop of the two-horse team's iron shoes and the rolling grind of metal-ringed wheels on stone somehow made the night's cold seem even more frigid.

Hitex aborted the idea of marching farther on. A warm fire and a pipe of his favorite tobacco in their sitting room at home suddenly seemed far more appealing. The welcome conversation with his wife would help to clear his head too. Her intuition regarding unexpected strife rarely missed the mark, and there was only one small detail of his life that he wouldn't share with her. So instead of turning left, he turned right at the next corner for the Old North Quarter. There his house stood next to the city's oldest stone church on a quiet street. He set off at a brisk pace, knowing in just half a Flaxon hour, he'd be there.

Had it been a clear night—and had he kept his intended direction—he would have seen the figure of Blackly emerge from the side street heading toward the tavern. As he walked on, Hitex was sure he heard the faintest dark laugh some paces behind. A quick check over the shoulder revealed nothing. The chilling wind of hours past dropped away in no time, and above, both moons pressed hazily through the breaking clouds.

End to the storm, he thought, looking up.

As the mist cleared, debris and roof shingles could be seen scattered on the ground here and there. The mess made the ordinarily clear streets look uncared for.

Maker was ill tempered tonight. He tossed a glance at the moons, thinking on the death of the bishop—clearly a murder, as all of them knew but were perfectly content to go on with the ruse. *Seems a few of us were out of sorts.*

The now soft breeze pushed the corn-mint smell of fire-bush needles being burned in the hearths of surrounding buildings—a smell that always reminded him of home when he was away on war campaign.

The last leg of his journey home came via an easy incline he'd walked for many a year. As he drew near the top of the rise, the cemetery side of the church could be seen. He saw two warmly dressed locals crossing his view from left to right. He recognized the husband, who saw him at nearly the same time and waved.

"Evening, Colonel. Good night to be indoors."

"Indeed, Mr. Blatchit. The fireside will be welcome," Hitex said.

As he said it, Hitex noticed the cobblestones of the street shining with reflected moonlight. The illusion made it appear as though they were walking on calm water.

"Evening, Colonel Hitex," said the woman. "Good night for quack-bills too, so hope we've seen the last of it now." She gripped the heavy shawl covering her head and neck.

Hitex tipped his hat slightly. "Missus Blatchit."

Everyone kept moving. Hitex saw his house in the mid distance and a light from a window on the east side as he began to pass the cemetery.

Wonder if Juni is still up?

That light always made him feel better. Just for a short time he didn't have to be a leader of armies and vanquisher of Flaxor's enemies. A small smile lined the corner of his mouth.

Home.

He saw the vacant bench in front of the church, and even as cold as he was, Hitex moved toward it. The wrought-iron fence barrier behind the bench partially obscured the well-maintained graves and tombstones beyond. It was a place he would often sit and think by himself. The bench offered a pleasant vista of Weirawind's rooftops. He slowed and removed his hat, choosing to sit for a moment before going inside. Brushing some remaining dribbles of rainwater from the bench, he sat with a sigh. He looked left and right. The street seemed empty in both directions.

Here, fine sheets of mist still lingered on the night air before turning to vapor. In the far distance he heard the ringing of the castle's funeral bell, signaling a death in the high court ranks. He saw some of the darkened windows of the houses below now slowly glow with lamplight. Close by, to his right, he heard the momentary sound of tinkling fine glass falling to the ground.

"Well, it's out of the bag now," Hitex said to himself, looking away to the east end of the road.

"You're right about that, Colonel," came a long-forgotten voice from behind Hitex.

The voice and its proximity startled the colonel, and he twisted around his seat trying to see who'd spoken, but he couldn't make anyone out in the misty darkness.

Hitex still recognized the voice easily enough, so he gave a little smile and then nodded. "We both agree, it's been a rough one tonight. No mistake there, eh, Dogg? But the storm's gone now. Should see better things in the morning."

"My thoughts exactly," came a second voice.

Now the colonel's mouth dropped open in amazement. "It can't be. It's been an age since you both—I mean, since we last spoke."

"And far too long, my old friend," said the second individual who now took a seat next to the colonel. "We did say we'd look in on you from time to time."

By all appearances the man sitting next to Hitex was a well-dressed Flaxon officer, a major by the pips on his collar. About fifty or so turns of the Flaxon yearly calendar. Tall with uncharacteristically dark skin for a Flaxon.

A distant memory surfaced in Hitex's mind of times past, trying to place the voice with the man he saw sitting on the bench. "Where did you come fr—"

Hitex cut his words short as his eyes darted left and downward upon seeing movement there. At the officer's feet sat a stocky, small gray dog unlike any of the breeds common to Weirawind. In a blink he also remembered her with fondness.

"Miss Tula—I mean, Dogg," Hitex said.

She looked up at Hitex with her deep blue eyes, tail fanning the ground. "That is I," she said in an accented tone that also sounded highly educated. "Hello again, Colonel."

Hitex touched a very small lump behind his ear and remembered back long ago to when it had been placed there. "Ah, yes, I suppose it is," he said softly.

The officer watching the dog's interaction with the colonel lifted his view back to Hitex. From under the officer's forward wedge-point of his tricorn hat, Hitex saw and felt that unforgettable cobalt-eyed stare and white-toothed smile.

"It's good to see you again, Colonel. It's been quite awhile."

Hitex looked from one to the other. "Uniss . . . Dogg. It's really you? Until this moment I never expected to see either of you warden profilers again after our last exchange." Hitex looked at Dogg. "Are you well, Miss Tula? I hope you no longer have the ailment you received from that terrible event with the Scarzen." He looked at her face caringly. "Has your ear healed well?"

"I'm fine now, Colonel, thank you."

Hitex then stared at Uniss's tricorn hat. "And your . . . unusual friend—he's still with you?"

Uniss looked up toward his headwear. "It's okay, Trev," Uniss said. "We can trust him."

From near the top of the hat's crown, Hitex watched two large sapphire-blue eyes slowly blink open.

"Trev goes wherever I do," Uniss said.

"Ever since you introduced me to the Jenaoin," Hitex said, "I've not looked at a single hat the same way."

Trev said nothing and slowly closed his eyes once more.

"Well, heartfelt greetings to you all," said Hitex, smiling.

Uniss tossed Dogg a glance. "They're both kind of hard to get rid of, to tell the truth."

Dogg offered a feigned growl.

"Settle down, Dogg. Just jokin'." Uniss lifted Trever's brim so his black curly hair, face, and dark eyes were better exposed. "You've got that 'world falling down around your ears' worried look, Ferdinand. How's your daughter?"

Hitex's demeanor brightened. "Right and bright as sunlight since the incident. Mereany's legs healed like you said they would. After you pulled her from the ice, we thought she would never walk again. That was years ago now.

She's grown into a fine young woman." Hitex paused and smiled again. "She's to be married soon."

"Really?" Uniss and Dogg said in unison.

"That's wonderful, Colonel," Dogg said.

"Great news," Uniss said. "Hope the best of life rolls her way. Who is the suitor, may I ask?"

"A fine young officer in the engineers, named Soams—Lieutenant Soams. You met him near Mereany's accident. He remembers nothing of you two of course. All of it has me in your debt."

Uniss and Dogg looked at each other solemnly for a moment.

"Yes, we remember him," Uniss finally said. "Your daughter chose a straight and noble one, that's for sure. He has an interesting future ahead of him. His replaced memory of events will keep him safe."

Hitex nodded. "I've said nothing of our commitment to my Juni either, as you requested. It's the only secret I have from her."

"It's for the best, Colonel," Dogg said. "The fewer who know you are in our employ, the better."

Hitex noticed the calm that had settled all around them in last moments. How unusually quiet it had just become—until the church bell behind them broke the silence again. They looked behind to the church tower for a moment.

Hitex sighed. "It didn't take them long." He looked at Uniss. "Suppose you know about the strife at the castle this evening, then?"

"Yep," Uniss said.

Hitex grimaced. "There was something truly evil about that business tonight. I've seen death often during my time, Uniss—some of it necessary, all of it tragic. But tonight was the first time a death struck me to the core." He eyed Dogg and then Uniss. "Is that why you've come?"

They both looked away and stared off.

"It's connected to that," Uniss finally said. "Every time an innocent is taken off the grid, especially on this world, we have to investigate."

"You should know," Hitex said, "that cad Blackly mentioned a very strange character—he called him Starlin—operating in the shadow of the regent's interests."

"Thought so," Uniss said. He scratched his neck and then frowned. "That's not good."

"You asked me to watch for any arcane activity out of the ordinary in your absence," Hitex said. "The business tonight, in my view, fits right into that frame. The way Blackly spoke of this Starlin and the apprehension he demonstrated—something is wrong about the whole thing. Blackly is not easily shaken. I don't know why, but I felt it was significant to mention."

"It was—very," Dogg said.

Uniss pointed at an approaching procession heading up the rise toward their position. A dozen or so senior priests of the Church of the One flanked a royal death cart. It was drawn by two black mares regaled in black glider eagle and dancing sigrat feathers.

"That's from the excitement at the castle, by the looks," Uniss said. "Dogg, go take a peek, would ya? See if there's anything of interest. Keep an eye out for you know who."

"I'm on it."

With that, Dogg headed off for the deeper shadows, padding silently down toward the procession.

"There's some big trouble coming this way, Colonel—big. If you see Starlin, stay right out of his way." Uniss pointed casually to the colonel's ear. "Your UT acts as a beacon of distress if you tap it three times. Do that and I'll be on my way."

"Very good, thank you. And how would I know what this Starlin looks like?"

"Sorry, forgot. I explained last time, but I had to give you a memory suppressor to keep you safe. You'll know Starlin the moment *he* finds you. But in case you do get to spot him first, he always wears a long brown leather coat, fedora—umm, that's a smallish hat with a mid-crown and medium brim. And he always wears a pair of shiny brown boots."

Thinking, Hitex remembered something else. "My sources gave me some threads about odd murders in the south. In Old Gantry Town, they said. I also overheard Magistrate Waldon in conversation with one of his agents about the strange deaths of Scarzen that had been encountered there. That seemed related—the wounds indicated a thrusting weapon, and the wounds had all turned to stone. I overheard that exchange courtesy of the improved hearing you bestowed on me—last time, wasn't it? I was going deaf as a post before then."

Uniss patted the colonel on the shoulder. "It's worked out well for both of us, Ferdinand."

"I did speak to Waldon of the Scarzen matter," Hitex went on. "He didn't seem surprised somehow. Said he'd look into it. Nothing has come back, though. I wondered if it could have been a Celeron battle mage who'd done the killings."

Uniss shook his head. "Nah, my friend. There's only one blade that'd do what you're describing, and it doesn't come from this world."

Hitex looked shocked. "You didn't do it, then?"

"What? Oh, nah, not me. Let me rephrase: there's only one *other* blade on this world that could match mine, and it's carried by the one we're tracking—Starlin. We're only interested in him and the great catastrophe we believe he intends bringing to this world and many more if he succeeds."

Hitex's mouth dropped open. "If what you say is true, he must have unimaginable power."

Uniss shrugged, then thumbed the silver-and-gold pommel of a long sword clipped to his belt. "He's been sloppy. Normally leaves no trace."

Pausing, Uniss thought, *Was it on purpose?*

"Must have been in a hurry," the colonel said.

Uniss looked at Hitex. "Listen well, Colonel. If you see Starlin, you stay well clear, hear me. He's very, *very* dangerous, and nothing the likes of you folks possess has the power to take him down. He wouldn't think twice about skinnin' you all alive if it suited his cause. Just tap on your translator three times and leave the area fast as you can."

Hitex nodded.

"Anything else I need to know?" asked Uniss.

"Well, there has been some spying going on near the new weapons foundry. Specifically the guarded foundry where the new heavy fire-iron artillery is being developed."

Uniss looked right at Hitex and smiled. "You're building cannon now! I only made the comment last time in passing as a jest when I saw what you were using against the Scarzen."

"We may be primitive by your standards, but Flaxon are resourceful. With what you gave us, I had my bell-caster, Screwshot, and the master fletcher work together. They came up with a forging process based on your descriptions of the weapon. We are happy with the progress thus far."

"Struth, never thought you'd actually get there. How did you discover the recipe for the gunpowder—I mean, black powder—anyway?"

"One of Waldon's agents happened to turn a disgruntled Celeron alchemist. His knowledge of the black flashing powder—he called it that—was traded for sanctuary here in Weirawind. Apparently he'd managed to attract quite a price on his head in the Celeron Kingdom . . . Bon City, I think. He needed to disappear—fast. His knowledge of metals and the arcane has proven useful in many ways. Once the powder's power was harnessed, the next steps to make it useful to our military weren't difficult. That young Soams I told you about before, he has quite the flare for testing and upgrading weapons in the field."

The procession they'd been keeping an eye on now approached, stopping on the opposite side of the church. One of the priests, in a very tall hat, began to chant as a cluster of pallbearers carried the coffin inside.

Both Uniss and Hitex kept facing each other as if chatting.

Once the procession had gone inside, Hitex sighed. "Our regent's mishap with the bishop this evening will have great consequences for all Flaxor. Strange how he died. Appeared more like an act of vengeance to me."

"I'll look into it when we return from Gantry Town," Uniss said. "Might be a good idea if you sent your family to somewhere like Bon City. Safer there."

"Flaxor has always had its measure of trouble, Uniss," Hitex said. "And my Juni will not leave her home or her husband's side."

"Try to convince her otherwise, Ferdinand. There's a war stirrin'—a war the likes this world has never seen. Flaxor's going to have a front-row seat and have to survive the aftermath. It's why I have to find Starlin."

"Can I help?" Hitex asked.

"No. After I find and deal with him," Uniss said, "we'll be back. Then it will be time to begin. Hopefully we can stop the trouble before it starts."

He doesn't look hopeful, Hitex thought.

"You take care, Colonel."

The sound of horses approaching from the right made Hitex look away. A short distance from them, a night patrol on horseback plodded their way. The officer leading the patrol on a well-groomed chestnut seemed to recognize Hitex and stopped the patrol, saluting.

"Evening, Colonel. Bit cold and bleak for a lone look at the Maker's sky tonight, isn't it?" The officer looked up. "Come to think of it, I suppose the stars pushing through will stay. Are you alright, sir?" he asked, looking back to the colonel.

"Uh . . . I . . . uh." Hitex wondered why Soams hadn't acknowledged Uniss's presence as a Flaxon major. He snapped a glance to the bench space beside him, only to see Uniss still sitting there. Then he looked back at the patrol and found they'd all frozen in their respective positions—as if time itself had stood still.

Hitex looked back at Uniss, who winked at him.

"Remember what I said, Ferdinand. War's coming. Starlin is dangerous. Wait until we return."

"Noted," said Hitex, nodding.

"Colonel Hitex," called the officer again. "Are you alright, sir?"

Hitex looked back to the patrol to see everything was normal again. Clearing his throat, he looked up at the officer awkwardly. "Ah . . . yes, indeed, Lieutenant Soams. Didn't expect to see you making rounds for the night-watch yet."

"A favor for a comrade ill equipped to sit in a saddle tonight," Soams said. "Too much tipping of the amber, if you take my meaning."

An extended pause filled the gap. Lieutenant Soams took the moment to look toward the colonel's house with interest. Hitex knew it had nothing to do with him.

"I see," Hitex said, clearing his throat again and bringing Soams back. "Well, don't let me keep you. Vagrants will be out now that the storm has cleared."

Lieutenant Soams pinched the front tip of his tricorn hat in salute. "I bid you well, sir," he said and then urged his horse on.

Hitex watched the five mounted soldiers pass, still amazed at how Uniss could be sitting there next to him and yet totally invisible to anyone else. Suddenly, though, Hitex realized that Uniss had vanished altogether.

Hate it when he does that.

"You best go inside, Colonel," came a soft feminine voice to his right. "It isn't safe out."

Hitex turned to see Dogg standing there, staring at him. Nodding, the colonel stood, obedient to her request. Tipping his hat in respect, he moved on toward his house as Dogg stalked off silently in the opposite direction.

CHAPTER

4

Dark Deeds, Small Blessings

Weirawind City awoke the next morning to a chilly but dry, cloudy day. The terrible storm of the night before was long gone, but it had left much for the street sweepers and bin carriers to clean up.

After taking a discreet look inside the church where the bishop's body now lay, Uniss continued his search for Starlin. He knew Starlin would still be in the area to finish whatever nefarious mischief he was up to—none of which would be good for this world. During the moments he'd spent watching and listening from the cloisters inside the church, Uniss had overheard discussions of a celebration of the bishop's life. Somehow Starlin had managed to have a hand in the bishop's death, Uniss felt certain. The celebration would happen in the city's central square. Everyone would be there.

"And so will Starlin," Uniss muttered to himself. "Better get down to the city square quick smart."

***

By the time Uniss arrived on the outskirts of the city square, maiden flower-dancers had already begun their all-day vigil and citizens had started gathering. As per Flaxon church protocol, a Special Honor holiday had been declared for the passing of the One God's highest representative. Town criers walked the streets ringing their bells, calling all of Weirawind to take part in the celebration.

As the law dictated, all Weirawind citizens would attend—and there would be merriment. Horns and sloop strings would be played.

Any citizen found in breach of obligations would be labeled as malingerers and prosecuted under freeloader law for sullying a Weirawind privileged citizen's name. All would be put on town clean-up duty immediately after the celebration. They would then be sent to serve in the fields to help bolster the produce for the regent's city silos. Only paid soldiers on patrol or guarding the city walls were exempt from such festivities or prosecution.

Standing on the edge of the large square, Uniss watched a growing gathering of citizens dress the town square for the ceremony at seven bells. They strung flowers along every second-floor balcony. Others hung Flaxor's gold-trimmed heraldry next to church banners displaying the symbol of a sun cradled in a crescent moon against a white background. From the vertical posts down to ground level hung garlic bulbs and sprigs of jessop bush to encourage Bishop Targus's spirit to watch over Weirawind. On the edges of the square, citizens set up temporary stalls where clink would be exchanged for celebration fare.

Uniss hid in plain sight in his Flaxon military garb, moving slowly amongst the citizens. He kept to the square's perimeter. Starlin, he knew, was also a master at concealment in plain sight. In fact it was his favorite method of assassination. Uniss had tracked him across many worlds and alternate realities, cleaning up one timeline after another in his wake. Scanning the square from rooftop to cobblestones, Uniss found that Starlin was nowhere to be seen.

I know you're here, Uniss thought. *What are you up to, Starlin? What's your endgame?*

Across the other side of the square at the corner of a side street, Uniss noticed that a cute little girl and her mother had just set up a stall. They'd hung some flowers and birds in cages. On the ground at the little girl's feet sat a broad basket. The sign in front of it said: *Puppies for sale.*

Uniss thumbed the knot on the back of his ear to activate his universal translator's secure short-range channel. "Dogg, see anything?"

A flutter of white noise fizzed across the comms as he waited. Finally her choppy reply filtered through: "No. . .ing yet. I'm on the opposite side of the squa . . . to you. Look up."

Uniss scanned the square's buildings.

"Second-story roof. Three smoki . . . chimneys above th . . . guest hou . . . on the gable.

In the distance Uniss saw her silhouette next to one of the chimney stacks. "Right, got you. He's here, Dogg. I can feel it."

More white noise flooded the comms as Uniss looked for Starlin.

"I've been . . . Tryin . . . to call y . . . for the last twen . . . minutes. He must be close by. I saw . . . St . . . n in . . . regent's . . . any. Think he spotted me. He's using a rogue comms jammer."

From the side street next to the stall with the puppies, Uniss noticed an individual in a long dark brown coat and fedora-style hat approach the woman. Uniss frowned, watching closely, his intuition warned of impending trouble. He felt a knot in the pit of his stomach.

"Stall to the north. Flowers and puppies. See it, Dogg?"

"Got it. Uniss, that looks like . . . lin."

Some words were exchanged between the woman and her customer. The customer remained with his back to Uniss and Dogg's view as the woman directed him to the little girl and the basket of puppies. The little girl first shook her head in response to something the customer said. More words were exchanged. Finally the little girl nodded.

What's he up to? Uniss wondered.

"Get over there. Someth . . . not right," said Dogg.

As he moved forward, Uniss watched the little girl lift one of the puppies out of the basket. She handed it to him with a smile. Clink was exchanged, and the customer put his head down and appeared to be cradling the puppy for a moment. Then Uniss saw the customer look directly at him long and hard over one shoulder. *Starlin.* It was indeed him. Uniss increased his pace, intending to confront Starlin, who gave him a momentary malicious smile. He handed the puppy back to the little girl. It suddenly looked very limp. Then he strode off into the shadowed ally.

Bastard!

As Uniss approached the stall, the little girl let out a scream.

"Eeeee! Mother! The puppy is dead! He murdered my puppy!"

All attention nearby focused on the stall and the crying child as Uniss drew parallel to them and stopped. He caught a glimpse of Starlin's figure disappearing from sight in the shadows.

"I'll find . . . rlin," said Dogg. "Help them."

Uniss knelt in front of the little girl, who was now being consoled by her mother. She looked to be about ten turns of the calendar old. Upon hearing the ruckus a gathering crowd began to close in to see what had happened. Uniss knew why Starlin had committed the heartless act, and knew all the attention Starlin meant for it to have. Uniss had no choice. An innocent life had been taken. Something had to be done fast before the animal's good karma and influence were drained away and lost.

"Ma!" cried the little girl, cradling the puppy in her arms.

"How could the brute be so callous?" asked the little girl's mother.

As tears streamed down the little girl's face, Uniss reached out with both hands toward her.

"Please, little miss, let me have a look. Maybe I can help."

She looked into Uniss's eyes and, feeling the urge to comply, gently handed him the pup.

"He's killed, sir, and no mistake," she said in a ragged voice.

Uniss took the pup carefully.

"I even heard the little bloke's neck go *crack*," the little girl cried.

"Aww!" said some of those in the small gathering.

"Where is the mongrel?" someone else shouted. "Should have his shins well and proper tapped with a good piece of timber!"

"What's your name, little miss?" Uniss asked.

"Elea Wax, sir. Moon Face was the special one in the litter—he really was."

Huddled close to Elea, with the wall on his left and her mother blocking the view on the right, Uniss slipped the pup inside his thick coat. He gently crossed his arms as if he might be cold for a moment and smiled at Elea.

"You know, young lady, that was a bad thing he did. Very bad. He'll be caught and dealt with, don't you worry—I promise. You know, I think he might have just frightened the little fellow. Sometimes if we say a little prayer, small blessings can come our way. Help me, okay? Close your eyes and think of him fondly."

Elea shut her eyes, but then peeked a bit. Staring at Uniss's chest, she saw a small golden glow from inside his jacket. Her eyes opened like bright pearls. Two breaths later came a small whimper.

Uniss reached into his coat and pulled out the wriggling puppy.

"Moon Face!" Elea said. "Oh, sir! However did you do such a thing?"

Uniss smiled and handed her the pup as some of the onlookers clapped and cheered.

"That's such wonderful magic, sir," Elea's mother said.

"Nah. It just wasn't his time," Uniss said, looking at her. Then he turned to Elea. "I think you are right: maybe this one *is* special. Should keep him, I think."

Uniss and Elea's mother exchanged glances. The mother nodded and mouthed, *Thank you.*

"Oh, yes, sir," said Elea. "He'll stay with me forever, and all the others will have a good home too."

"Just remember little one," Uniss said as he stood up, "forever is a long time, so feed him well."

With murmurings amongst the curious on the rise about what had just happened and fingers pointing his way, Uniss left the scene. Only when he'd entered the alley in pursuit of Starlin did a much more serious expression cross his face.

"That one you'll pay for, old mate, and it'll go hard on you when it does," Uniss whispered.

CHAPTER

5

Get Starlin

Heading along the alley, Uniss followed Starlin's last seen direction, tapping his translator a little ways in. "Dogg? Have you got him? Do you have Starlin?"

Uniss waited for a reply, but heard only white noise over the comms. Searching through the west side of Weirawind, he tried the comms several times. When no reply came at all, he began to feel concern. On a side street he found a ladder that took him to the rooftops for a better view. In the background the bishop's afterlife celebration went on to the sound of bells, drums, and horns.

"What now, Trev?" Uniss said through his mind-link with Trever. *"Where the hell has she got to?"*

"I don't know, Uniss. If her short-range comms aren't working, perhaps we might get a ping from her on-world signature."

Nodding, Uniss pulled a small scarab-shaped device from his pocket and held it flat in the palm of his hand.

"It's worth a try." He looked at the face of the device, which now read: *Tracking. Designation—Warden Tula.*

The scarab glowed jade green and finally pinged. Uniss waited for the miniature holo-map to form, but none appeared.

"It's malfunctioning," Trev said.

"Must be the rogue jammer."

Then Uniss sighed in frustration and said aloud, "No detail at all, but I do have a distance and bearing."

Instead of the usual miniature map of the surrounding landscape, a segmented yellow band of light pointed the way forward.

"She's outside the city walls," Uniss said. "Southwest of here."

"I can locate her faster by myself," Trever said.

"Nah, Starlin would want that. Makes us easier to pick off. Best stick together for now."

"Are you sure it's really *her* signal? Could be a misdirect."

Uniss shrugged. "Not a bad thought, but all I can say is that it's definitely her ping. Come on. We've got some ground to cover."

***

After leaving Uniss in the city square, Dogg couldn't know separating them had been Starlin's intention all along. He'd led Dogg on a merry chase, just long enough to lure her into a trap. She'd followed him into a dead-end alley, intending to apprehend him. Instead Starlin blindsided her using a micro cavion-field grenade. The small stasis field it emitted held her frozen with a surprised look on her face. The field stripped her of all her warden powers, which allowed Starlin to soul-core transport her against her will beyond the city limits. So moments after her capture Dogg found herself miles from Weirawind, southwest in the forests of Flaxor. When she rematerialized, she found herself perched on a tabletop like a trophy. She appeared to be in the main room of a large country house.

Where am I? she thought, fighting through the haze of her clearing mind. *A Flaxon structure from the look of it.*

When the fog of her eyes had cleared fully, not only did she see Starlin standing there, but another familiar and formidable enemy as well: Zharkaa, the traitorous former commander of the elite Scarzen security force in Brasheer Mountain. At nine-foot-nine, and still showing the scars from the failed coup against Farron Bach's Brasheer warriors, Zharkaa was a menacing, imposing sight. He had to stoop to stand under the support beams holding up the roof of the building.

With the shutters on the outside of the building locked, light inside the open plan house was supplied by four paraffin lamps: two hanging from the exposed beams of the A-frame that formed the ceiling skeleton, and one on each wall at opposite ends. To Dogg the shadows cast by the lamps in the ceiling gave Zharkaa's features a demonic air. He no longer wore the heavy drommal-hide armor of the Scarzen elite forces he'd once commanded. His coverings were now the same burgundy as those of the rebels who had attempted to usurp Farron Bach's authority in the Brasheer Mountain several decades ago.

"Not someone you expected to see?" Starlin asked with that patronizing tone he loved using with her and Uniss.

Not in a millennium, Dogg thought, unable to respond verbally due to the restricting cavion field.

"As you can see, he is no longer in exile and is here with a full contingent of Dark Scarzen clan, now loyal to me."

Zharkaa stepped forward, looking upon Dogg with deep-orange eyes that showed cold vengeance. "I want to hang her head on my wall," he said to Starlin.

Dogg felt both anger and true concern for what the appearance of Zharkaa meant. He was also the individual responsible for removing her ear tip and trapping her in her present guise. Zharkaa smiled at her, something that meant only pain where any Scarzen warrior was concerned. He looked back at Starlin as though wanting some sort of acknowledgement.

"Alright, then," Starlin said. "Have your say. You earned it."

Zharkaa stepped even closer, his substantial form looming over Dogg. "You once scarred me, Warden," Zharkaa said. He traced a fingertip over the disfigurement that ran from under his right eye to the corner of his mouth. "You and your allies with Farron Bach may have thwarted my mission's success to help liberate our race from the slavery you have imposed upon us. But I have returned with my warriors, the true servants of Scarza, to exact revenge. Our ally, Agent Starlin, intends to see our aim achieved."

He presented a closed hand to Dogg, as if to offer something. Slowly turning it palm upright, he opened his fist to reveal her missing ear tip—the ear tip he had sliced off in his skirmish with her in the last moments of their struggle for control of the mountain. Looking at Zharkaa's gruesome war trophy, Dogg felt a combination of rage, frustration, and elation. There it was—the one thing she needed to return to her true form. Without it she would be trapped in her canine disguise forever.

The moment I am free . . .

"Now I have scarred you and you shall carry that scar for an eternity," Zharkaa went on. "Agent Starlin tells me this is the key to you becoming whole again. This I keep with me always as a reminder." Zharkaa placed her ear tip in one of his utility-belt pockets and then looked to Starlin. "I still want her head on my wall."

Starlin smiled and moved to the hearth off to Dogg's right. In it the flames burned low. He warmed his hands and said, "That's a pleasant thought, my friend. The Dark Scarzen deserve true justice for how they were betrayed. But I'm afraid her purpose in our success must reach further than the mere satisfaction of her demise. I think you will find what I have in mind just as pleasurable."

Dogg could see only one way out of the building: via a door that led outside to her left. With the door partway open, she was sure for a moment she glimpsed another Scarzen just outside.

Starlin left the fireside and moved to sit on a simple chair in front of her. He stared, wearing a smug smile. "You know, Tula, I'm so pleased for the great disservice you've done me. In a way you and Uniss showed me the truth of how misguided the House of Zero is. Now I have the protection of Evercycle Three. Not having to deal with all that red tape, all those checks and balances, is so liberating. What was it all for anyway, hmm? Three was right. All we succeeded in doing was hamper the balance of the time-space Continuum."

Starlin straightened in his seat, gazing at her. He allowed an awkward moment to fill the gap.

"Oh, I'm sorry. You can't respond. Here, let me help you with that."

He pulled a warden's tech sphere from his pocket, a tool all wardens carried —about the size of a tennis ball, divided into many panels. He manipulated the sphere skillfully with his fingers, puzzle-cube style, for a moment. Then he looked at her, thumb poised over one of the many small pads.

"Now I know you're upset at being bested . . . again. Don't feel bad. I've always been smarter than both of you dull-brained minions put together. Play nice or I'll have to stiffen you up again and process you without a proper good-bye."

He pressed the pad with his thumb. The intensity of the cavion field imprisoning Dogg softened. Although still trapped, she was now able move her mouth to speak.

"You're insane, Starlin, you know that? You—"

Starlin pressed the pad again, and Dogg's mouth froze again.

"Yes, that was your testimony at my trial. The trial where you both threw me to the Hell Realms along with Lord Herrex. The trial that had Evercycle Zero try to have me banished to the Echaa Realms—FOR FULL ERASURE!" Starlin took a breath to calm himself and spoke again through gritted teeth. "You lost me my position as Citadel karmic accountant. Yes, I remember very clearly." He pressed the release pad again.

"You gave us no choice, Starlin. When you began your madness, Uniss and I tried to talk sense into you. Pigheaded as always, it had to be your way or no way. You were trying to open a portal for the Echaa to enter the Superverse common mortal life stream. Naught's beard, Starlin—*the Echaa!* A life form where a word like *diabolical* needs to be amplified to a power of one million to come close to making their description possible."

Starlin waved off the comment. "So you say. Both of you were always shortsighted! I had everything under control."

"Control? You call what you were doing 'under control'? Are you talking about the part where you erased tens of thousands of innocent incarnate timelines across a thousand worlds? Or the part where you prevented several key individuals from being reborn on worlds that needed their presence to advance their civilization?"

Now Starlin flinched, but he said nothing.

"You were playing god to the extreme, Starlin. The only interest you had was self-fulfillment. Three should never—"

"I was playing at nothing!" snapped Starlin, thrusting himself to a standing position. "Three! Don't implicate her in this. *She* was the only one who stepped in with clear eyes to see what my real intentions were. She saw how things really were and knew I understood a better way! *She,* unlike you two, spoke for me from the pulpit in my trial. Lord Zero refers to you two as his 'golden avengers.' He always singled you out, even when our efforts were aligned. I was never included in his praise. Three understands me, and the potential I have to further the Superverse's greater cause. You and Uniss denigrated me in that trial. ME —Starlin! The one who saved both your necks on so many occasions! We were allies and you watched me burn."

"Do as you wish to me, Starlin. The Superverse will implode before I lift one finger to help you in your mania. What are you really on Tora for anyway?"

Starlin's shoulders slumped and he sighed. "I always liked you Tula, so I'll tell you why I'm here." He leant toward her, his expression shifting to represent the extremely cold, psychopathic murderer at the core of his nature. "There'll be an entirely new Superverse order when we're finished, I can promise you, and it includes the total destruction of the House of Zero."

Dogg looked from Starlin to Zharkaa. "You think you'll get access to the Brasheer Mountain via me, don't you?" Dogg asked. "You're sadly mistaken. What has he promised you, Zharkaa—world domination? Or perhaps a way off this world? Or is it the *Tome of Zharkaa* and a united bond with Hex, which he knows is impossible?" She looked back toward Starlin. "If you want access to the sub-gate, Starlin, you will be sadly disappointed. Zharkaa and his warriors destroyed it in the skirmish."

"Hex himself promised me liberation, Warden!" Zharkaa snapped. "I am no one's servant. My warriors and I ally with Starlin because he showed us the truth of your and the Mistress Farron's treachery. The tome and all it contains is mine! You and your infidel allies stole it. We will recover the tome and take the mountain for our own and set Scarza back on its correct destiny."

Dogg looked again at Starlin, who stared back at her blankly. His silence said it all.

"You've been played, Zharkaa," Dogg said. "How do you know he does not have the tome already? Starlin does nothing unless it's exclusively for his benefit. Even if your combined efforts managed to breach the mountain's first defenses, you'll have to face Farron and her Brasheer inside. You were crushed after trying to ambush her in a cowardly way, Zharkaa, remember? Back then, you had surprise on your side and an attack from behind. You'll not catch her off guard in such a way twice. She'll especially look forward to dealing with *you*, Zharkaa. Your actions are not that of a patriot. You are a traitor to your kind and a disgrace to those you pledged to protect."

Dogg's final remark apparently struck Zharkaa sharply. He drew a claw-bladed dagger from a scabbard on his belt.

"I'll have more than your ear this time, Warden," Zharkaa said. "Let her free, Starlin. I'll finish what I started—only this time there won't be enough left to fill a peasant Flaxon's clink sack."

He went to step toward her, but Starlin extended an arm to bar the way.

"No no, my friend. Not that way. It's what she wants. We need everybody present for the party to begin." Starlin smiled at Dogg. "You are wrong as usual, Tula. I think the cache of PCGs I have will even up those odds in the mountain nicely."

"You're bluffing," Dogg said. "Personal cavion grenades were outlawed by the Jenaoin High Command and Evercycle Council after the Corsel Incident. That was two centuries ago."

"Were they? *All* of them?" Starlin asked.

"All stockpiles were either destroyed or stored in the Fortress of Bach. Uniss and I saw to it personally."

Starlin grinned and pulled one of the small cylindrical smart grenades from his coat pocket and showed it to her. "You mean like the sample I have here?"

Dogg gasped.

"I had the chance to glean a full unregistered stockpile *before* the manifest was released to you. I have them hidden in substantial number throughout this M System sector and in the ethereals. I even have some of those terribly nasty little split-spectrum gems. The type that the Varian military cloned from stolen

Jenaoin FM tech originals . . . before they took part in the Corsel Incident. Clever bunch for mortals, those Varian. Whom do you think Evercycle Five put in charge of the program to carry out your signed order? Slipping the Varian the schematics before my arrest felt so good, and all done right under your nose."

"You're twisting everything," Dogg said.

"In truth," Starlin went on, "it was because of Uniss's and your incompetence that we achieved the circumstance needed to facilitate my escape from that holding cell in Juno."

Dogg squeezed her eyes shut in frustrated anguish.

"I'm sure my Lord Herrex is watching events now with some enthusiasm. Now all I need is a sizable swath of my lord's trilix heart crystal. The entire damn mountain is full of it in each bunker in fact. Then we'll be ready for phase two. And you, dear Tula, you are going to help me get it."

Tula managed to form a frown. "No chance!"

"If you refuse," Starlin said, "I promise you'll hear the screams of your loyal Uniss from Tora to the Dimension of Death's Reach and Gray Ghosts by day's end."

A noise drew Starlin's attention. He and Zharkaa both turned and looked through the gap the open front door provided of the outside world. Dogg intuitively followed the direction of Starlin's gaze. Just outside, next to the door's right shoulder, the partial profile of another dark-clad Scarzen warrior could be seen.

"What is it?" Starlin asked Zharkaa.

Using his mind-tether to speak to the guard outside, Zharkaa turned his head to one side as if someone was whispering in his ear. When the message from outside had finished, he looked at Starlin.

"Nothing. Just some wildlife being flushed from the underbrush," Zharkaa said.

Starlin brought his attention back to Dogg. "You're probably wondering why I've told you so much."

"Because you are a longwinded wannabe autocrat with delusions of grandeur whose only true interest is himself?" Dogg said.

Starlin's jaw dropped. "Wow, Tula. I had no idea you felt that way. There are a dozen cavion traps around this hovel for starters. Some look just like trees or even ordinary rocks. One or two of them are black hole traps—you know the ones—and others are matter dispersers. If that isn't enough of a challenge for Uniss and his Jenaoin, a full unit of Dark Scarzen—armed with a variety of my personal choice ordinance—are concealed just outside. Even Uniss's warden skills will find that proposition steep to overcome. If he navigates around them, I'm going to fracture your memory using your dear Uniss to trigger the event. So even if your hard-charging friends make it inside here, you'll be of no use to them at all."

From his other pocket Starlin pulled a Varian split-spectrum grenade and placed it on the table directly in front of Dogg. The domed-shaped explosive had a tiny green flashing light that faced her.

Starlin waved a hand toward the grenade. "It's on a proximity timer, as you can see. It will begin its countdown the moment they enter the building." Starlin then looked back outside via the doorway. "Uniss has undoubtedly tracked us down by now, as intended."

Now Starlin turned back around and tapped the grenade with one finger. "In short, this will hurt, a lot, forever. Unless—well, it's decision time, Tula. You know my word in such matters is good. So what's it to be—help me or oblivion for you all?"

Dogg said nothing in answer to his ultimatum, but Starlin knew he was getting through. Dogg's stomach turned summersaults of anguish. She knew

Starlin hated Uniss, even worse than the contempt he held for her. He intended pure vengeance this time for sure, a magnitude nothing short of something Mephistophelian.

"What?" Starlin said. "You thought I failed to notice your little deception of splitting your tracker signal back in Weirawind? You are so predictable."

Dogg looked at the spectrum grenade sitting in front of her. Depending on the level of ordinance it contained, she knew it had potential to vaporize half the building.

"Uniss will beat you, Starlin, and he won't be gentle like last time when he just killed the drive on your ship."

Starlin smiled. "Soon, Tula, I'll win—you'll see. You should at least save Uniss. Give me the voice signature that opens the stronghold doors into the Brasheer Mountain and you have my word he'll be left alive."

"Is that all?"

"No. Second, there is no way you destroyed the ethereal mortal node sub-gate in the mountain. I want the new location and its activation signature."

Dogg kept her eyes closed, making Starlin wait for her reply.

"Come on, Tula. My patience is at an end. I know you both moved that EMN somewhere nearby under a camouflage field, no doubt. Where is it?"

Dogg opened her eyes slowly. "Drop this field and I'll give you my answer, Starlin."

Starlin sighed and tossed Zharkaa a glance. "Zharkaa, give your warriors final orders." Then he looked back at Dogg. "You know, Tula, we really were good together once. I'd hoped you'd see reason. I would have forgiven you, eventually."

"It's you who should seek forgiveness, Starlin. Lord Zero *will* send you to the Echaa Realms for this. You won't escape a second time. Throw yourself on his mercy. Countless timelines and worlds will cease to exist if you attempt any reversal of Lord Herrex's present position."

As if on cue a solid gust of wind struck the side of the house.

Starlin looked about the walls. "Hmm, he doesn't seem to agree." Starlin pressed the mute pad on Dogg's cavion field control sphere. "Some things must be sacrificed for the greater good, Tula. Your end will be for a good cause. It's time for you three to be retired—permanently."

Starlin rose and went over to the door, then pulled it wide open to make the view clear. "There. That should give him ample perspective of your predicament," he said, one side of his mouth twisting into a smirk. "Let the games begin."

With Zharkaa standing beside him, Starlin reached to press the button on the center of his long coat, activating their soul-core transfer.

"Good-bye, Tula. Give Uniss my best."

The forms of Starlin and Zharkaa became translucent before vanishing in an upward thrust of an energy stream, leaving Dogg in the house alone.

She looked down to see the grenade's flickering green light shift to a steady pulsing orange.

It just armed. Gods, let them stay away.

CHAPTER

6

Living on the Edge

On a brush-covered slope a short distance from the country house, both Uniss and Trever looked at the open front door with keen interest. They saw Dogg imprisoned under a cavion field on the table inside. A single Scarzen sentry stood guarding the front door. A sentinel by build, he wore the heavy burgundy leather armor identifying them as part of the Dark Scarzen rebel faction.

"Trev, how are Dark Scarzen here on the mainland? When they were exiled, Starlin and I put Zharkaa and his cronies back on a boat to their island of origin across the Shalane Ocean. He was supposed to escort them back and lock the island off. That must have been the point when Starlin flipped on us. What in Naught's beard is he doing with them here?"

"Nothing good," Trever said from his usual vantage point on top of Uniss's head.

"And how many are here? Can you see Starlin? This could start a full-scale Scarzen civil war with him bringing them back to the mainland."

"Switching to life-force vision," Trever replied.

"Thought I saw another Scarzen inside," Uniss whispered.

"No one in there now," Trever said.

Uniss frowned. "I couldn't be sure; they moved off to the side too quick. Are you certain there's no one else in there now? There's only one way into the place, unless they put a back door in since last time I visited."

"Whoever it was isn't in there now."

"First question: Is it a trap?"

"You know it is."

"He wants us all in there, Trev, that's for sure. What does he hope to gain sneaking back here to Tora?"

"Don't know, but the Superverse is now divided in two fundamental regions, so it's a delicate balance. One endless ocean of galaxies in multiple dimensions, bound by time, gravity, and strong and weak force. If I were Starlin and I wanted to create a major disruption to the balance of things, Tora has elements that would make such a venture possible."

"Yeah, but for what purpose? Why is Starlin meddling in the affairs of Weirawind? And where does Trabonus fit into all this?"

"Good luck with answers there."

The Scarzen guarding the door moved to the end of the building, drawing Uniss's and Trever's attention.

"Uniss, I just completed a wider sweep with life-force vision, and I detect three other Scarzen life forms, aside from the obvious decoy keeping our attention. They've all applied their blur skill to conceal their positions around the cabin. To the north, the first one is secreted in foliage twenty degrees to the right in that cluster of thick underbrush."

"Seen," Uniss said.

"The second is in a tree lookout position. Look left of the house. There is a large forked stendle tree. They're camouflaged high in the branches, carrying a heavy war bow by the looks."

"Got 'em."

"The third is hidden in plain sight using a contour of stone to blend in. Look to the two large boulders—right side of the house, about fifty feet out."

"Got 'em. That's only four total. Their units normally number five. Where is the other one . . . and why spread so far apart? This isn't a conventional Scarzen battle circle, Trev."

"Starlin understands well your familiarity with Scarzen combat. He will not want us to play to our strengths."

"He never wants us to play to our strengths, Trev."

"Will you want me to function in defensive or offensive capacity?"

Uniss sighed, then went back to their mind-link. *"Go defensive, Trev. Knowing Starlin, they have orders to kill everything in sight. We'll save them if we can. Scan for tech traps."*

"Acknowledged."

From Trever's brim a membrane of cool green energy enveloped Uniss.

"Adjusting vision detection to search for concealed threats . . . I detect three devices external of the house. Danger category, unknown. Definitely radius-trigger ordinance, though, by the pulses I'm seeing. One of them looks exactly like a small tree; the others mimic stones. We'll need to approach the house from the left."

"Right, then. Time to do a little sneaking of our own."

Uniss pressed the left side of the symbol on his belt buckle with his thumb. Trever's defense field shimmered, and any light contacting the two of them now bent to perfectly emulate their surroundings. The result made them effectively invisible to all life natural to the Toran world.

"Okay, Trev. Let's go get Dogg. Just don't forget what happened last time."

"You were running and took evasive action before I could warn you."

"You're plugged into my brain as much as I am. Compensate."

"Roger that. Remember, once we begin moving, head out too fast and the one at the door will see the spatial distortion. Then the rest will know our position in an instant. Being former Brasheer, these Scarzen have very keen senses when it comes to change in their environment."

"I got it. Keep my hands and feet inside the vehicle at all times. . . . Trev, you listening?"

"Roger, sorry, thought I saw . . . Never mind. Bear northeast, then direct to the door of the cabin. Your safety corridor will be narrow, to less than one shoulder width by halfway. Your step triggers the dead zone. See that log directly ahead? Careful there. A life form's inside it."

Uniss moved forward carefully, placing his complete trust in Trever's light-spectrum vision as he had done in countless fixes of this kind before.

"Ten steps ahead, steer left of that log. One of the trap fields is overlapping it."

Advancing, Uniss kept one eye on Dogg and the other on the Scarzen in plain sight. He moved like a fugitive in a spaceport trying not to be noticed. As he passed the far end of the log, the life form inside it moved. Next to his down-treading boot, the head of a large hornbrow adder slithered into view. The weight of his boot broke a stick, and one end of it slapped the reptile's jaw. It hissed and shied away. The action forced the snake directly into the path of the trap. In a blink a sizzling sound of static began, and the first third of the snake vaporized like a burning fuse. Uniss breathed a sigh of relief that it wasn't his leg that had been vaporized. Facing directly toward the Dark Scarzen guarding the door, Uniss saw the intense focus that the warrior now gave their position.

"Freeze," Trever warned. *"The trap is still in flux."*

A few tense moments later Uniss heard the familiar retracting sound of static as the trap auto-reset. He glanced down to see the headless snake body lying limp next to his boot and a charred line where the rest of it had been.

"That was a CSM," Trever said.

"No kiddin', Kermit? Where did he get bloody cavion spectrum mines from? Starlin's playin' for real this time, Trev." Uniss's full attention suddenly swung to Dogg as a realization hit him. *"Oh no! Trev, get us over there fast!"*

"We can't increase the pace any further and stay concealed. Everyone is watchin' this position now, especially that one at the front door. He'll move photon fast if he gets a sniff of us closing the gap. Starlin will likely have ordered her executed at first sign of us."

"Not while she's under that cavion field . . . Nah, wait a minute. Starlin isn't letting us see her so easily for nothing. Trev, when I say 'Go offense,' that's your cue to grab the attention of those on our periphery. Cover some ground; put on a bit of a show. Don't kill 'em, mind you, unless you have to. I'll deal with the one at the door."

Uniss watched the guard at the door relax his posture and then turned to check on Dogg again.

"Okay, Trev. Where to from here?"

"Go twenty paces straight to that round stone, and then flip sideways over that fallen branch. You'll have to stick the landing in two steps. Move straight on, and then follow the track that leads to the front door. Get that far, and you're clear of the last barrier."

"You mean except for the blade-wielding doorstop in the way."

"You love a challenge! You'll be fine. Only thirteen paces more to the door."

"Just don't get us caught in a pincer again. The scar on my shoulder from our last sojourn is still healing."

Uniss centered himself again with a steady deep breath and then stepped off. He arrived at the round stone without incident, completed the side flip, landed silently, and gave the order: *"Go offense, Trev."*

Trever dropped his defensive field. His eyes dilated to six-inch sapphire-blue burning discs and he lifted off Uniss's head. Their separation made Trever visible and an immediate target while Uniss remained concealed. Unable to move quickly without being seen, Uniss felt it took an eternity to close the gap to the Scarzen. Almost there, Uniss shot a look to Trev's position. The Jenaoin had placed himself equidistant between the two Scarzen on the right flank and began hurling energy volleys at them to draw their attention.

Uniss swung his view back to the doorway. The Scarzen there now had filled a hand with a cruel curved long knife. The hair on the back of Uniss's neck stood up.

I'm seen!

The Scarzen engaged their blur skill and charged in Uniss's direction, hurling repel barriers with their free hand. The Scarzen's second volley caught Uniss in the shoulder, disrupting his camouflage field and almost toppling him. For a moment Uniss became completely visible. From his left heavy war arrows shot by the Scarzen lookout sizzled past his head. Two struck the ground only a step ahead of his now charging advance. Another two set off mines to his left, one making the surrounding stone turn to lava.

At Trever's position the other two Scarzen attempted to route him, moving in close for the kill. To pave the way, they hurled repel barriers like energy-seeking missiles, which forced Trev to evade them like some mad wasp. Returning a volley of his own, Trever managed to stun both of them. He turned in time see Uniss, god-cutter blade drawn, slip past one vicious cut from his much larger opponent and reply with a slash of his own that missed. Goading the Scarzen to lunge, Uniss evaded the committed stroke, dragging his own blade through the Scarzen's inner thigh and severing the limb completely. The Scarzen arched back and cried out in agony, then fell face-first with a thud to the ground. Uniss didn't stop to ensure his fallen enemy was dead; there was no time. He rushed through the doorway.

"Uniss, stop!" shouted Dogg, looking at the tabletop in front of her. "Spectrum grenade!"

"How long?"

"Seconds—I don't know."

Uniss shot a look outside. "Trev! Get in here!" He ran to the table and looked at the grenade. "I don't know that color. How big is its radius?"

"I don't know," Dogg said.

"Trev! Stop playin' out there. Need you in here NOW!"

Trev came crashing through the roof like a small meteor to hover directly over Dogg and the explosive.

Uniss pointed at the grenade. "Dogg's cavion field—can you disarm it?"

"Only if you want me to set that ordinance off! Their pulse is synchronized."

"Hell with it!" Uniss said, picking up the grenade and running for the door.

Trev rushed forward too and jammed himself onto Uniss's head, casting his defense field down over them both.

"Uniss, NO!" Dogg yelled.

Just outside another Scarzen was charging at the door.

"Catch!" Uniss said.

He tossed the grenade at the surprised warrior, who caught the explosive skillfully just as Uniss ducked back into the house and slammed the door shut. Then Uniss drove a determined shoulder hard against the door. A short moment later the sharp electric whip-crack of the grenade's detonation accompanied a thundering shockwave that struck the building. Most of the door and part of the wall in front of them vaporized. The blast left Uniss and Trever with a smoking carbonized layer that had once been the door between them and the outside. With the smell of ozone filling the air, Dogg watched the smoldering matter tracing their outline remain suspended for a moment. As they relaxed, the converted matter fell to the ground at Uniss's feet as black sand.

"That could have been all of us!" Dogg snapped. "What were you thinking?"

Uniss blew an exasperated breath, looking at her incredulously. "Trev, get that thing off of her."

A small pulse of energy left Trever's eyes, striking the cavion field. The room filled with a quickly escalating sharp pitch, and the field around Dogg suddenly sizzled and evaporated. Dogg slumped forward and staggered about on the table top for a few steps.

"Don't mention it," Uniss said. "Should have left you to be pickled by Starlin's little gift, then!"

Dogg shook her head, trying to shake off the giddiness. "No. I . . . I meant . . . you could have been killed."

"Sorry to break up the friendly reunion," Trever said. "But her molecular integrity has taken a beating after being eroded by that cavion field. She needs to be stabilized."

"What! Is she alright?" Uniss asked.

"I'll be fine," Dogg said. "Stop talking about me like I'm not here."

"She seems to be fine," Trev said, ignoring her. "At least that's the feedback I'm getting from my visual scans."

"I'm fine," Dogg said, looking about and trying to focus her eyes. "Just a hell of a headache, that's all. How in Naught's beard did I get here?"

Uniss eyed her. "What do you mean, how did you get here? What did Starlin want?"

"Starlin?" Dogg looked at Uniss blankly. "Is he responsible?"

Uniss rolled his eyes. "Oh, great. Yes, he is, and the unnecessary dead outside."

Dogg shook her head back and forth, her tongue lolling. "It's all jumbled bits, sorry. Last thing I remember is chasing Starlin into an alley in Weirawind."

"Hm," Trever said. "He must have set the field to memory shock in the event we did get to her in time. She'll remember scraps of things at best. We need to get her off-world and back to the med bay for thorough examination."

"What's that on the table?" Uniss asked.

He reached to pick up a small metallic disc near Dogg's feet. The moment he touched the device, the voice of Starlin began: "So if you are hearing this, you're still standing. Disappointing. As always, I've bested you three again. The next one will be our final round."

The recording ended abruptly.

"Hmph. Ego the size of a planet," Trev said.

"What does he mean, the 'final round'?" Dogg asked.

"Never mind that now," Uniss said, looking at her with concern. "You look like you need a hand."

"I'm solid. Let's go." She leaped off the table, only to land drunkenly on her chest and face in a heap on the ground. "Well, maybe not."

"That's my thinking," Uniss said. He knelt down and picked her up in both arms. "Come on, old girl, let's get you looked at. Trev, contact Central."

"Acknowledged."

"Don't worry, Dogg. Starlin will pay for this. We'll be back in no time. There is big stuff going on here and we'll get to the bottom of it."

The universal translator behind Uniss's ear blipped, then he heard, "Warden Uniss, this is Central. Bringing you home now, sir."

A broad column of silver light enveloped them all and retracted skyward, taking them with it.

CHAPTER

7

Conspiracy Rising

In the hours after Bishop Targus's death, the court of Weirawind Castle became embroiled in intrigue and pandemonium. With the unscheduled ringing of church bells in the early hours of morning, in no time at all Weirawind City was awake.

A hunt for the malicious murderer was announced by castle and town criers everywhere. In the streets church investigators, accompanied by members of the RHS, began knocking on citizens' doors. Someone had to pay for a crime of this magnitude, and they *would* be found. While the hunt continued, the church's wailing women of Flaxor gathered inside the Royal Cathedral in the south quarter. Their task was to cry up a storm for the bishop's passing before the crowds gathered. Monks and interpretive scholars of Hex's Word soon gathered inside the cathedral to recite from his text and pay respects. By full daylight devout citizens of Weirawind took vigil everywhere, praying for the bishop's righteous passing and the forgiveness of Hex.

In the castle Inquisitor Hatchet, as new head of the church, had been summoned from his bed. In the Royal Chapel, still in his bedclothes, Hatchet presented a hastily prepared sermon. The small gathering of court officials mourning the passing of the bishop were accompanied by Regent Trabonus and Magistrate Waldon. They sat in the front-most pew, looking suitably saddened over the loss of their dear friend.

"How long do we have to be here?" Trabonus whispered out of the corner of his mouth.

"Shut up and grieve like you're supposed to," Waldon whispered back.

In the far background the incessant banging on doors for inquiry carried on.

***

On the castle grounds a facile investigation had begun, personally carried out by Terrence Blackly and his RHS—Waldon having ordered Blackly to forget their earlier plan to announce the bishop's death as due to an accident: "We need to hang this on someone to appease the people," Waldon had said, with Trabonus's blessing, of course.

So, from the top step of the castle's main entrance, Blackly addressed his agents: "Mark my words, lads. Leave no door unchecked inside the city. Every agent will report in by sundown. Hex will smile on none of us until the culprit is found and brought to justice."

The agents dispersed rapidly to begin their investigations. Not long after, many reports from God-fearing citizens stated in whisper that Hex had become displeased with some of the bishop's less-than-priestly activities. Some believed Hex himself had struck down Bishop Targus. Notes were taken, and the RHS agents paid comments of "Thank you, sir. I'll take it under advisement, sir." Other damning reports said that the bishop had been part of a coup to have Regent Trabonus deposed. Hearing this, Blackly personally found such reports amusing, but no real cause for concern—although he made it sound as if it was.

Sitting at his desk inside his cluttered office, Blackly heard a knock at the door and called out, "Enter!"

The door swung inward, and a castle footman stepped into the room. "Sir, Magistrate Waldon requests your presence in the War Room."

"Very well. Tell him I'm on my way."

***

A short time later, entering the War Room, Blackly saw he was the last to arrive. The group of co-conspirators all turned to watch him enter. A servant was pouring each guest a mug of hot cacklevien tea from a silver pot. Sitting in his regent's chair and looking much more composed than in recent hours, Trabonus waved the servant away.

"Come in, Blackly. Sit down," Trabonus said. "There is much to be set right."

Blackly did as ordered. He felt a rare tension in the room and wondered at what might have already been put into play. Most of all he wondered what Starlin was now doing behind the scenes.

"Well, what a bag full of offal this is," Trabonus said.

"That's putting it mildly, my lord," said Hitex.

"There'll be a scandal," said Waldon. "The church inquisitory is demanding a private audience with you, my lord—to, ah . . . ascertain the facts of the matter."

Trabonus flushed scarlet at the comment. The newfound strength Blackly had seen when he'd first walked in had vanished.

All it took was one word from Waldon and his lordship is jelly again, thought Blackly. *I'll have to watch myself 'ere.*

Waldon had the tiniest hint of a smile that disappeared faster than the fleeting moment it had appeared. Blackly saw it, though.

"They *will* want a conviction," Waldon said, setting his hot beverage down after a sip. "No stopping that."

"Well, what do you all intend to do about it, then?" Trabonus snapped.

"Don't see there's much we can do, my lord," Waldon said, seeming to enjoy the moment immensely.

Trabonus began to shake his head. "Oh no you don't, Waldon. If I go down for this, you're *all* coming with me."

"Well, my lord," Waldon said, "I'm not sure that's—"

"A redirect," Blackly said, cutting Waldon off.

"A what?" Trabonus asked.

Blackly looked at the regent. "A redirect, sir. A patsy, a stooge . . . someone the church inquisitory will enjoy focusing more on than you."

Waldon sat back in his seat, his momentum temporarily interrupted. "Hm, I suppose that little black book of secrets you guard so closely is about to offer up something juicy to save the day, Blackly?"

"As matter of fact it can, sir."

"Well then, don't hold back, Blackly. Let's hear it," Trabonus ordered.

"Yes, my lord. There is a certain officer of the Royal Guard who shares, or rather shared, a consort with our dearly departed bishop."

"Surely you're not implying . . ." Hitex said, trailing off.

"As it happens, I am, sir," Blackly said. "I think implicating one Lieutenant Banister and his secret love, Courtesan Heartflower, in this crime will fit nicely. I think blackmail-gone-wrong is a far more believable bone to throw the inquisitory than just some random assassination. Courtesan Heartflower and Lieutenant Banister obviously conspired to compromise the bishop's position by having him caught in a moment of weakness. But the bishop refused to comply, forcing Lieutenant Banister to act. A struggle ensued and our dear bishop met his end. The inquisitory will be eager to seize upon such an obvious transgression against church doctrine. At worst they will defend the bishop's integrity and provide a suitable offering to satisfy both doctrine and Flaxon law."

Hitex folded his arms over his chest. "Careful now, Blackly. You tread a very fine line. My officer's integrity is beyond reproach. Nobody will swallow that. Lieutenant Banister has been decorated three times by his lordship for valor on the battlefield in recent times—including once for a daring rescue of several soldiers under his command cut off by a Scarzen patrol on our southern border. These are *not* the actions of the criminally minded."

Waldon gave a sharp nod. "I suppose it's also mere coincidence, then, Blackly, that they are the same two who served as witnesses implicating *you* in high treason four seasons ago? The same Lieutenant Banister who is also my and your lordship's third cousin?"

"As you know, sir, those charges were disproved unequivocally," said Blackly, raising a placating hand. "I and the two officers implicated were acting under the specific instruction of his lordship." Blackly gestured to Trabonus. "I was instructed to root out the evil dealings of an insidious spy ring serving the Celeron duke, Talcalus. Licentious behavior amongst those, even within the noble ranks of our fare Flaxor, has raised its wicked head in the past. This situation is no less believable."

"No chance in all this that you're trying to clean up some of your own dirty business, Blackly?" Hitex asked.

"Sir, you shock me with the insinuation. My first concern, as always, is the welfare of my lord regent."

"Gentlemen," Trabonus interrupted. "In these difficult times hard decisions must be made for the good of our people. It is unfortunate that such a decorated soldier has lost his way, but I'm afraid things must be put right. Blackly, have an arrest order issued immediately for the culprits."

Colonel Hitex shook his head, clearly uncomfortable with the story of betrayal by one of his bravest officers.

"They'll be in custody within the hour, my lord," said Blackly.

"What of the courtesan? She is innocent and well thought of by the aristocracy," Waldon said.

"It is a mask all females wear well," Trabonus said. "She will be executed along with the disgraced officer. Hand them over to the church inquisitory and have them committed for trial. Put this matter behind us as soon as possible. Inquisitor Hatchet's ascent to position of high bishop will be formalized in a public ceremony on the morrow. Have him come to my chambers as soon as possible."

"As you wish, sir," Blackly said.

"How will we now prove the act in question *did* indeed occur as has been portrayed by this fantasy of yours?" Waldon asked. "While avoiding the inquisitory's knocking at our own door?"

"I approach them first with impeccable witnesses such as ourselves, sir, to ensure the eyewitness accounts are flawless," Blackly said. He looked to Trabonus. "If I may, my lord?"

Trabonus nodded. "Go ahead, Blackly."

"My records shall tell that you discovered the terrible scene when you had need to make a late call upon the bishop regarding a private matter. Thereafter you raised the alarm, and, being in proximity, Magistrate Waldon and I came to see what all the commotion was about. His lordship ordered an investigation, and I promptly found good reason to suspect the guilty parties. I requested an arrest warrant be issued."

"Yes. That seems to be all that's needed to be discussed, I think," Trabonus said. "I'm sure you all have things you need to attend to. I shall be in my chambers."

Everyone stood, following Trabonus's example, and as he left for his chambers via a side door, the others departed via the main entrance. Looking quite surly over all that had transpired, Waldon strode out of the War Room first.

Hitex, though, stopped Blackly at the door. "You really are a cad, Blackly. I won't forget this."

"I'm sure you won't, sir," Blackly said. He nodded and left without engaging any further.

CHAPTER

8

Conspiracy

Leaving his former allies to an intended miserable end, Starlin returned with Zharkaa to their secret base of operations on Tora. Located on Ludd's west coast, in the Wild Lands, the hideout's location was virtually inaccessible by physical means. If anyone did manage to get that far, then the only option for any mortal seeking entry was to descend by way of an unfathomably deep sinkhole. A narrow slaa-thread ladder dropping some hundred and eighty feet restricted access to one individual at a time. At the bottom a small ledge led to the mouth of a dimly lit narrow passage. There, several paces in, two Dark Scarzen shock warriors always stood guard. Anyone not possessing the password immediately found themselves ejected, back into the abyss.

The "Nucleus," Starlin called it. Even by Evercycle Council standards for secrets, it was hidden well, right in plain sight under the Council's nose.

If not for Evercycle Three speaking on Starlin's behalf at the Jenoa War Trials, his erasure alongside Herrex, Lord of Balance, would have been certain. To ensure the correcting of Superverse balance, certain harsh steps had to be taken, Starlin believed. The Nucleus had been set up for that specific purpose. He'd manage to establish the base shortly before his fall from grace. Only Evercycle Three and his small loyal band of Dark Scarzen subordinates knew of its location. Built in a subterranean labyrinth of caves, the Nucleus spread through a vast maze of tunnels made of pure black trilix crystal. The Dark Scarzen were healed and invigorated by the environment, just by standing in it.

Black trilix was all but unknown to the greater population of Scarza, including the bunker high keepers. For them only one kind of trilix existed, and that was the less pure blue variety. As commander of the Brasheer warriors in Brasheer Mountain, Zharkaa had answered only to Farron Bach, one of Starlin's former allies. He'd made a valuable asset for any Scarzen power play.

They now materialized in the Heart Chamber of the Nucleus. Upon leaving a small raised platform used for receiving soul-core transfers, Starlin and Zharkaa moved immediately to a console utilized for off-world communication. An artificial light source from above—not understood by the Scarzen—illuminated the console's many small screens and domed control interface.

"With our strongest enemies now out of the way, what is the next move, Agent Starlin?" Zharkaa asked.

"Don't underestimate those three," Starlin said. "They have a habit of defying the odds. I must speak to my lady to ensure that their demise is final."

Starlin focused on the console and began skillfully tapping on sections of the central dome with a knowledgeable rhythm. With each touch the part of the dome his fingers contacted blinked with light.

"This should get straight through, but the security encryption on the other end is being changed randomly."

Starlin finished his operation of the console with three taps of a finger on a small screen to the right of the main dome.

"There. Now we wait for her response. Send a scout to see if there's any news of reinforcements landing on shore. We have to be ready to act at a moment's notice."

"It shall be done," Zharkaa said. The Scarzen then turned away to speak to a subordinate on the other side of the chamber.

Starlin had a small smile to himself watching the giant tower of a Scarzen move off.

I wonder what my Lord Herrex really intends for you?

Starlin had secured the services of Zharkaa and his allegiance some time back when he was commander of the Scarzen Brasheer. He'd divided the solidarity between Zharkaa and his superior, Farron Bach, by creating a division of trust. To do that, Starlin simply saw that a leaf from Zharkaa's tome expressing doubt over Farron's linage and rite to command the Brasheer was placed where she would find it. It didn't take long before Zharkaa realized he was being watched and resented it.

That position made it easy for Starlin to meet with Zharkaa and show a sample of black trilix and by extension expose the truth about Hex.

"All Scarzen have been lied to from the beginning," Starlin had told him while handing Zharkaa a vial of the onyx liquid. "What I offer you is Hex's heart—and the truth. Sample this and know for yourself."

Once Zharkaa ingested the black trilix, the rest was easy. Shortly after Starlin's liquidized offering was swallowed, dreams of Hex's voice and a direct connection to the Lord of Balance began for Zharkaa. That experience had convinced Zharkaa to lead the nearly successful coup and demise of Uniss, Dogg, and Farron Bach in the Brasheer Mountain. Starlin had observed all that unfold from afar. The coup might have failed, but the observation of seeing his former allies suffer had felt liberating.

Suddenly Starlin's console began emitting a wistful chime and he came back to present happenings. A living bust of Three, Lord of Chaos, phased into a three-dimensional yet translucent image. For a moment she seemed disoriented, and then seconds later her emerald eyes found him and she pressed her full focus upon him.

"Starlin. This better be an improvement on our last interaction. Having to weather the trials of your failures is becoming tiresome."

Starlin only gave her a smile. "A pleasure to see you as always, my lady. I do have good news. Uniss, Tula, and that interfering Jenaoin, Trever, are by now cosmic dust. I am confident we can proceed to phase two of your plan."

"Is that so? Well, the three bodies in the Great Meeting Room speaking to Evercycle Nine's administrator looked perfectly healthy to me a bit ago. Your work is getting sloppy, Starlin. I don't know why I ever saw the need to make myself vulnerable in front of millions on your behalf." She glared at him. "I've bought you some time . . . again. The fully conscious Uniss and Tula are now on their way to Earth."

"What? Why?"

Evercycle Three sighed and rolled her eyes. "To chase down another dead end I've managed to throw in front of them. Some human plucked from the redundant pile of reincarnates."

Starlin took a deep breath, first because the wardens were still alive—which wasn't a major surprise to him—and second because he knew he'd have to move his own plans for independence forward.

"Thank you, my lady. Your assistance, as always, comes at the quintessential moment. I will see to my duties here and then deal with them permanently."

"See that you do. We are running out of time, Starlin. I can't keep them all blindsided for much longer."

Three's image evaporated, and Zharkaa approached Starlin from the right.

"Scout reports a full company of my clan have arrived."

"Excellent," Starlin said, feeling better hearing that news.

He smiled and thought, *Let the real game begin.*

CHAPTER

9

Epilogue

"So, Agent. Do you believe me now? What a state of affairs! Starlin no longer inspires confidence. He's up to something. But there is at least turmoil and intrigue on all the right fronts, which I can use. Citadel wardens running blind . . . mortals ready to die for nothing they can keep. Next time Uniss and his friends return, they'll be in deeper than ever. Can you see now, Agent? It's the coming of war. A war across the time-space Continuum in all its fine misery. They'll never see me coming."

***

What's this war that Three speaks of? Will Dogg recover her memory of Starlin's true intentions? And what will Starlin do next?

Find out why Uniss, Dogg, and their strange new apprentice from Earth must band together to prevent the destruction of all existence—this and more in further installments of the Citadel 7 Superverse by Yuan Jur!

About the Author

Yuan Jur served in the Australian military as a young adult. He later sought the solitude of monastic life serving the community as an ordained Buddhist monk for many years. In Buddhism's warrior-caste arm known in the West as Zen he achieved the rank of abbot and theologian. As a theologian, Yuan Jur studied many belief systems, doctrines and ideologies from around the world. During those decades he also gained a master's degree in Chinese martial arts and medieval weaponry.

In 2007 a life threatening illness ended his monastic career and nearly his life. During recovery, Yuan Jur turned to a new venture. He combined his knowledge gained from decades of belief systems study with a love of Time Travel Paranormal alt/world fantasy as a young man. The result was a totally new immersive superverse series called Citadel 7. By 2014 his first Citadel 7 series combined trilogy had won both blue ribbon and Grand Prize in the Chanticleer Cygnus international writing Awards. He states: "There is a lot, lot more to come."

9 780099 421531 4